Goin' to Hell: Fresh Kills

Volume One

Chuck Nasty

To Mom

PRAISE FOR CHUCK NASTY

"Is StonerGore a genre yet? If not, I think Chuck's claiming it!"
- Stephen Cooper -The Rot
"A fun rollercoaster ride of action-packed gore that reminded me of a Tales From The Crypt story on steroids! Chuck Nasty keeps getting better and better with each new release!"
- Otis Bateman, author of the Maggot Girl series and My Vice Is Your Unfathomable Agony.
"This is one fun horror thrill ride. It's art. A Novella told through connecting short stories! Chuck Nasty delivers."
- Chisto Healy – The Pit
"Fresh Kills is bubbling over with gore, horror, and humour—the most fun I've had with a
book in a long time."
- Sidney Shiv – Where Demons Dine
"Chuck Nasty strikes again with his riveting and gag-worthy story-telling! In these tales, he has created a character who will undoubtedly emerge as a formidable presence in horror.
With his unique style and delivery, he leaves readers shaking, bringing a double dose of pure defiance. GOIN TO HELL: FRESH KILLS VOL ONE is a delightful journey you cannot miss. It's a wild fucking ride!"
- Dan Shrader, author of SOULLESS LONESOME.

GOIN' TO HELL: FRESH KILLS

CONTENTS

THE WAKE

"A shame, really. He was such a good man," an elderly female voice said to a woman sitting next to her on the pew. The woman shook her head and agreed. Just then, an elderly gentleman sitting behind them leaned forward.

"He sure was!" the man said quietly. "He always made sure that my family was taken care of, as well as many others. Just a real shame."

"It's true! Whenever he came into the diner, he always was a big tipper," a woman in her late thirties said, joining the conversation with tears in her eyes.

Conversations such as these went on throughout the funeral home. Men and women of different ages were gathered. They all spoke about the good deeds of the old man in the casket.

"Good afternoon, everyone!" A man dressed in black slacks and a black dress shirt said as he stepped up behind the podium. "I am quite impressed with all who showed up today." He paused and looked at a notebook sitting on the podium.

"Excuse me! Where is Reverend Johnson?" A woman in her mid-thirties hollered, confused.

The man in black looked up from the notebook, staring the woman dead in her eyes, and chuckled. "In due time, my dear. In due time. I know you all are here to pay respects to this man," he said with a raspy voice, then pointed to the casket. "Thomas Jenkins!"

It was obvious that many sitting in the pews were bewildered by what was going on. Some weren't interested in why Reverend Johnson wasn't there. They just wanted to get it over with so they could go on about their day. They only attended because it was just what you did out of respect for someone in a small town. Nonetheless, everyone in the room found themselves intrigued by the man in black's presence.

"Let me continue by saying that some of you are going to hate this service and some of you..." He hesitated. "It won't affect you in any way." The man in black grinned. He looked back down at the notebook, reached over to his right breast pocket, and pulled out a cigarette.

"Excuse me! I hope you're not planning on lighting that!" An older woman in the front row hollered.

The man in the black placed the cigarette in his mouth and raised his eyes to meet the woman's. He gave her a grin, and the end of the cigarette lit up on its own. Her eyes widened in horror. Others who saw the same thing gasped. Bible-thumping men and women started praying, afraid the man before them was no man at all.

"Now, everyone, just relax and calm down! Everything will be explained shortly," the man in black said, raising his hands and waving them back and forth above him. He created a tiny tornado from the endless stream of smoke pouring from his nostrils.

"I don't like this, not at all!" A heavy-set man with a bushy beard stood and quickly sprung for the exit. He didn't get too far. The double doors to the viewing room slammed in his face as he was about to walk through. "Hey!" he shouted.

"Not so fast, Billy Fisher!" The man in black took a drag of his cigarette and blew the smoke in the man's direction.

"How-how did you know my name?" Billy Fisher asked as he stood at the doors.

The man in black laughed. "Don't be such a fool! Take your seat, and let's get this over with. Shall we?"

Billy Fisher quickly went from looking frightened and confused to fucking pissed. He balled his fists up and walked swiftly toward the man in black, who stood at the podium with his arms to his sides, grinning from ear to ear.

"I guess we can go ahead and get you out of the way first," the man in black whispered to himself.

Everyone noticed that Billy Fisher was no longer charging at the stranger behind the podium. He stopped short and stood close to the podium at the front of the room. His face drooped, and his arms slowly raised on each side in a crucifixion pose. Suddenly, his arms jerked from their sockets. Billy screamed, as did everyone watching. The sound of his flesh and bone ripping from his body echoed throughout the room. Finally, his arms slid from his shirt sleeves and fell to the floor. Blood poured from the large cavities his shoulders once occupied, leaving huge puddles on each side of him.

He fell to his knees, exhausted. His mouth dangled open as crimson dribbled from every hole in his face. Tears leaked from his eyes, mixing with the blood that followed. Billy let out a painful scream, this time louder than before. His head twisted around farther than nature should have allowed before his neck issued a loud CRACK! Billy fell to the floor, landing face-first into a puddle of his own blood.

The room erupted once again with cries of concern and horror. The people in the pews looked at each other as if they all had the same thought: *try to leave!* But no one dared to move. Everyone understood they'd remain seated in their pews to avoid sharing Billy's fate.

"Holy Shit! I knew I should have made sure none of you could just get up and leave. Someone gives you free will, and you assholes really know how to abuse it, huh?" The man in black shouted as everyone took their seats.

"What are you going to do with us?" A woman in her late twenties, with her blonde hair put up in a green bow, inquired nervously.

The man in black smiled at the woman. He dropped his cigarette on the floor and stepped on it. "To you? Nothing," He replied as he stepped from behind the podium, walking down the aisle between the rows of pews. When he reached the woman, he placed his hand on her shoulder. "You're shaking pretty bad. I would say that this has been a traumatic experience for you. Am I right?"

"Yes." She replied, tears falling from her eyes.

The man in black smiled and wiped her tears away with his free hand.

"No need to cry. You're free to go," The man in black replied as the double doors opened by themselves. "And, no worries. As soon as you step foot from this building, you will not remember any of this."

The woman grabbed her coat from the back of the pew and headed through the double doors and out of the building.

"Wait a minute! Why does she get to leave?" yelled the woman who mentioned that Thomas Jenkins had been a good tipper.

The man in black walked back to the front of the room and stood behind the podium. "It's

simple. Look at where you all are sitting. If you are sitting on this side," he said, pointing to the right, "you are free to leave. I guess I should have mentioned that earlier." He laughed. "If you're sitting on this side," he said, pointing to the left side of the pews, "you aren't going anywhere!"

"But what did I do?" The woman asked with uncertainty in her voice.

"Alyssa Garber?" The man in black asked, looking down at the notebook and then back to the young woman.

"Ye-yes…"

"Poor Alyssa… just a lonely server at a piece of shit diner! Poor Alyssa… the one who is always the first to help her fellow man! Poor Alyssa… the part-time waitress and full-time whore and drug dealer!" The man in black shouted.

"I-I don't know what you're talking about. You must have me confused with someone else…" Alyssa's body language said it all. Her whole body shook as she nervously picked her lip.

"My dear, you and I both know I don't." The man in black stopped and looked to the right side of the room. Eight men and women sat in the pews on the right, clearly waiting to be allowed to leave. "I almost forgot about you, good citizens. Please forgive me. You may leave!" Everyone sitting on the right got up, hurried to the double doors, and walked out. The doors closed behind them when the last one stepped out.

"What did I do that was so wrong? What did I do to deserve being here?" Alyssa pleaded.

At that moment, the bright lights in each corner of the room turned crimson, and the windows went black. The room went from bright white to dark and red within seconds. Everyone in the room froze, intrigued by the horror unfolding before them—fearing their fate. Every eye

remaining in the room was fixed on the man in black.

"Now, I see I have everyone's attention…" The man said.

"Wait!" Alyssa Garber interrupted. "I wanna know why I am being punished. Yes, I sold my body. And yes, I even sold some drugs..." Her voice was less shaky. She was trying to stay as calm as possible, hoping to talk her way out of the situation.

"Drugs... which you sold to plenty of careless junkies, including one who was so careless, she left her stash out. Her young child got a hold of it and died. The way I see it, besides the many other horrible things you are guilty of, that one right there earns you a definite seat here." The man in black was silent for a few seconds as he flipped through the notebook. "You know what? Why don't you come to the front, Miss Garber?"

Alyssa Garber removed herself from the pew and slowly walked to the front. She found herself standing in front of the man in black and next to Billy Fisher's mangled body on the floor. Tears filled her eyes, and her body started shaking again.

"Walk over to that casket. Look down at that man lying there and tell me if it was all worth it?" The man in black ordered.

Alyssa was hesitant to step over Billy's body.

"Oh, I'm sorry. Let me get that for you." The man in black waved his hand down at Billy Fisher's body. It flew to the other side of the room, splattering against the wall. The battered carcass slid to the floor, leaving a dark, bloody stain dripping from the wall.

The man in black pointed the middle finger of his left hand down at the body in the coffin. "Now, look at him! Right there! I heard you say earlier that he was such a good tipper! Thomas Jenkins, everyone's favorite man of money!"

Alyssa went to the casket and looked down at Thomas Jenkins' corpse. She couldn't help but have flashbacks of when she'd first met him. He had come into the diner many years ago, and yes, he was a good tipper. Everyone wanted to work his table, but he always asked for Alyssa to serve him. She couldn't help it. She smiled at the thought of how nice he was in the beginning. He always paid her such beautiful compliments—the kind that would make any woman's knees start knocking. But it didn't take much to get her to insert a cock down her throat, anyway. His voice was deep and soothing when he spoke to her, always getting the love socket between her legs to drip. Like a slave, she would do anything he asked of her.

"I see what you're thinking. I see you smiling. How cute! Now, why don't you think about the less attractive things that old man was responsible for? Think about all the people he royally fucked over. Think about the many people who died at his hands or the hands of his goons. Like Billy Fisher over there." A flash of orange flame appeared in his eyes.

Alyssa remembered the rotten things he'd done to people, including her. She went from thinking about so many good memories of Thomas Jenkins to thinking of some of the shittier times that son of a bitch put her through. She could see in her mind the first time he called her to come by his house and how he smacked her around, calling her awful things for his amusement. She remembered how he would throw wads of money at her to make it all better. For years, she convinced herself that money justified everything.

She looked around the room and saw at least four men she used to party with. Thomas Jenkins had paid for her services with all of these men. He got off on watching multiple men have their way with one woman, not caring about what they did to her.

Everyone had a price, and Jenkins knew it. Alyssa wasn't the only female under his

thumb. She was just the one who was always in need of money. So, she always found herself running back to the old man.

Jenkins would agree to give her money but would always sweeten the deal, throwing an extra few hundred at her. When she would finally agree, knowing whatever he wanted wasn't going to be pleasant, she would show up at his place. Jenkins and his goons would be standing around, waiting like vultures. She would be led inside Jenkin's mansion. There would always be two men, one holding each of her hands as they walked her to a room at the end of a long hallway. Inside, the room was bare, with nothing on the walls, no shelves, just a bed in the middle of the room. As soon as Alyssa would get near the bed, the group of men would rapidly undress her. Each piece of clothing would be ripped off and flung to the floor. When all her clothing was off, they'd surround her. One by one, they would grope every inch of her flesh. Men would painfully grip her breasts, pinching her nipples until they were numb.

The truth of the matter was Alyssa had a reputation around town for being slutty, which got her into some irresponsible situations. Still, she had never been gang-fucked until Thomas Jenkins came into her life. The idea of having multiple partners at once used to make her gag. When she started seeing dick sucking and cum swallowing as her job description, she just treated it as such.

For hours, each man would have their turn inside Alyssa. It got to the point that she just felt bored and disgusted. Each time one of those perverted old men shot their load inside her, only to have another one pumped in—load after load until it poured out like an avalanche—she wanted to puke. But she got good at holding back the vomit.

Thomas Jenkins had so much fun watching her get used like a rag doll that he would sit

in a chair in the corner of the room and stroke himself. Usually, when his tiny pecker was hard enough, he would hop onto the bed, knocking other men onto the floor. Like a proud child showing an art project to their favorite aunt, Jenkins would wave his cock in Alyssa's face, which was usually caked in multiple layers of semen by then. Catching it in her mouth, like a snake catching a rodent, she would bob her head back and forth on the old man's rod until he busted in her mouth; it was an extra two hundred if she swallowed. The drugs helped numb the taste.

Staring down at Thomas Jenkins in his casket, reliving all the bad shit in her head, she knew what hate was—she knew she hated him. Yes, she was grateful for the money but wished she could have chosen a better way to live. However, those wishes never stopped her from doing terrible shit—neither did the guilt.

"Let's not forget about the drugs, Alyssa! Let's not lose focus on the reason you're here—why you all are here." The man in black stared deeply at Alyssa but pointed at the people sitting in the pews. "MONEY!"

"I-I don't want to see…I don't…" Before Alyssa could finish her sentence, the visions started in her head again. She saw the moments when wads of cash were given to her. She saw the times she bought the pills and the heroin with the money that was given to her. She broke down in tears at the worst memory of all—the time she sold a baggie of pills to an addict friend. She'd been holding her friend's child in her arms at the moment of the transaction. The child's eyes were so innocent and pure. At the time, all she'd cared about, as her friend paid for the pills, was money.

"Is this getting to be too much for you?" The man in black asked.

Alyssa, with tears rolling down her cheeks, looked at the man in black and screamed, "I

DON'T WANT TO SEE IT ANYMORE! I'M A WORTHLESS PIECE OF SHIT!"

"I'm glad you're starting to understand. But how about this for a final memory?" The man in black squinted his eyes and grinned from ear to ear. "Here's something you didn't see!"

Alyssa's face became pale, and her body trembled. What she saw in her head was, indeed, nothing she'd seen herself—only heard about. The images cycled through her mind like a flip book, showing the woman—her friend—she had sold the pills. She saw the woman nodding off, her child crawling on the floor. She saw the child grab the baggy and eat each pill like candy. The last image was of the poor child foaming at the mouth, eyes going black.

"Had enough?"

"Kill me," She requested. Her voice was no longer shaky, just drained. Her skin was turning a grayish green.

"Well, I wasn't expecting that so quickly." The man in black grabbed another smoke from his pocket and it lit itself as soon as it hit his lips. "Alyssa Garber! For failing to make good decisions in life, I give you...pain."

As soon as the man in black spoke, Alyssa Garber opened her mouth wide. Her jaw stretched past the point that a regular mouth could open. The sounds of agony hidden within her blood-curdling screams made the others around her start to cry.

The flesh from her head down to her feet turned a greenish-gray tint. It slowly began to slide from her bones. When the blood started to pour from her ears and nostrils, the man in black laughed uncontrollably. Her eyeballs slowly protruded from their sockets until they finally popped out and dangled in front of Alyssa's nose. When her body collapsed, it made a SPLAT as she hit the marble flooring, leaving a disgusting mess behind as her soul left her shell.

"Such a shame!" The man in black shouted with a slight chuckle. "Would you all take a moment to uncover your eyes and look down at this pathetic waste?" He pointed down at the bubbling gore of Alyssa that lay at his feet.

"Who's next?" He pointed at the remaining people in the pews, waving his index finger, deciding who to call next. There wasn't a dry person in the place. They were either sweating bullets or had pissed themselves out of fear—in some cases, both.

"Excuse me?" A man wearing a white button-up shirt and khaki pants politely called for attention.

The man in black looked at him, wondering what he wanted. "You do realize this is kind of a big deal, right? That all of you are here to meet some type of ill fate?"

"I figured as much," the man said honestly.

"Then why do you people keep wanting to interrupt me? You have seen that I am capable of speeding things up and taking care of you all at once." The man in black sighed.

"Yes. I am aware of this," The gray-haired man said soberly.

"Then what the fuck do you want?" The man in black's voice sounded raspier than before. His facial expressions had grown more sinister—pissed off.

"I was just wondering if there was any possible way for any of us to get out of this. I admit that I have done wrong by a few people in my life, and for that, I am quite sorry. There must be something I can do to save my soul," the man pleaded.

"Save your soul?" The man in black laughed as he walked down the aisle to where the man sat. "Save your soul?" he repeated. "Oh, James Wallace, there is nothing that can be done to save your soul! You may be one of the worst in this room! You sick and twisted fuck! Something

tells me that you only spoke up when you did because you were one of the men who participated in Thomas Jenkins' sick parties. Alyssa

Garber was everyone's favorite fuck doll." His sinister grin became a crooked smile.

James Wallace nodded. "She never acted as if she was uncomfortable. Most of the time, she'd laugh and seemed to have a good time..."

"Let me stop you there, Jimbo. You see, your words are mere excuses—excuses that are usually made by horrible men that rape. Also, let's not forget how doped up she was when you all would get down to business. Don't get me wrong, she was a piece of shit. But it doesn't help that you are part of the reason she became that way. And let's not forget the many other crimes against humanity you have committed. You've murdered men, women, and children. Your actions are responsible for family homes being set ablaze because they wouldn't sell to Jenkins. Your list is impressive. Unfortunately, it just means you're more than qualified for what is coming to you." The man in black slowly walked down the aisle and stood in front of the casket, stepping through Alyssa Garber's puddle of mush as he did. He peered down at the old man's body and rested his hands on the closed half of the casket.

"What are you going to do with me?" James Wallace asked.

The man in black turned from the coffin and looked around at the people left in the pews.

"I'm getting there, I'm getting there." He rubbed his chin and clicked his tongue against his teeth. "Maybe it will be easier this way."

"What will?" James asked with concern in his voice.

"Oh, I am just thinking out loud," The man in black replied. He raised his hands and swung around to face the remaining few. "I think, before we conclude, we must talk a little bit

more about Mister Thomas Jenkins," he said as another cigarette lit between his lips. "I think we all can agree that Thomas here had his good qualities, but he had way more shitty ones." His voice took the tone of a demented preacher, spitting out words and taking deep breaths between each phrase. "Brothers and sisters! We are here tod ay...uh... to say goodbye...uh... to a horrible, no-good piece of walking trash!" He stopped and started to laugh. "I swear, if I had a different profession, I could very easily preach some bullshit," he continued in his normal voice, his preacher parody concluded. "Anyway, everyone here had something to do with this tub of shit." He pointed at the casket. "Every one of you! Some of you helped him move drugs. Some of you helped him rape and murder—yes, murder! The list goes on and on. Honestly, it's a long list that I don't feel much like repeating..." He came to a pause. "...but, Mister Wallace, let's go ahead and finish you, shall we? Come here!"

With that, the man, in his fifties, wearing a white shirt and khakis, who was said to be the worst in the room, walked to the front of the room to stand before the man in black. He didn't put up a fight. "I knew this day would come. I didn't know when, and I sure as hell didn't think it would be at a wake. What horrible thing are you planning to do to me?"

When James Wallace spoke, it was clear he was ready to meet his doom. He walked to the casket and looked at his old employer's body. "Yes, it's true. I am responsible for many terrible atrocities against my fellow man, and most were done under this man's order. I know there is no excuse for what I have done. No reason to put the blame solely on him when I was of free will." He glanced at the man in black. "So, I will ask again, what are you going to do with me?" He asked calmly.

The man in black chuckled. "Oh, it's not what I am going to do to you."

"What do you mean?" James asked.

James was startled when something suddenly grabbed his hand. He looked down to see Thomas Jenkins' dead hand gripping his, tight enough to crack his bones.

"It's what he is going to do." The man in black replied.

James Wallace struggled to pull free from Thomas Jenkins' grip, but it was useless. He used his free hand to punch the corpse.

Thomas Jenkins' eyes opened.

"OH GOD, NO!"

Thomas Jenkins' other hand raised up and grabbed James by the neck, pulling his head into the casket.

The remaining people in the pews sat in their seats, shrieking and crying. They knew there was no way they were going to survive. Everyone could hear the sound of the corpse gnawing on James' face, hidden from view inside the casket—the sounds of teeth crunching bone, flesh being chewed off, even a belch. When James Wallace finally fell backward out of the grip of the hungry cadaver, everyone could see that not much remained of his face. His once-white shirt was a sopping red mess.

"Ladies and Gentlemen! Thomas Jenkins!" the man in black announced as Thomas Jenkins' body struggled to get out of the casket. The commotion rocked the casket until it toppled over onto the floor. People stood from their seats, realizing they were able to move. They ran for the door, making one last attempt to leave the building.

"Oh, God! He's getting up!" a woman in her late twenties, wearing a revealing black dress, screamed as she banged on the double doors.

"This can't be happening! None of this can be real!" the man beside her added.

The stranger leaned against the podium and watched as the corpse of Thomas Jenkins squirmed its way from the casket and crawled toward the small group of people trying to leave. James Wallace writhed on the floor, not yet dead. His face was half eaten, and so were his eyes. He sat on the floor, wailing in pain. The corpse slammed his fist into Wallace's chest and ripped out his heart, shoving it into his mouth. Blood squirted out like a grape, sealing James Wallace's fate.

"Get up!" The man in black pulled the corpse from the floor and pushed him toward the people who were trying their best to knock down or push open the door. The man in black leaned back against the podium, enjoying the carnage, his sinister grin stretching from ear to ear.

When the reanimated corpse of Thomas Jenkins got down the aisle and was right upon the small group, he reached for anyone near him. He grabbed one man by the head and slammed his face into the wall, leaving a bloody smudge as he slid down to the ground.

The corpse grabbed the woman who had screamed out and was first at the door by her breast. He squeezed her tit so hard his fingers penetrated it. With her breast in his grasp, he leaned in and bit her throat, tearing out muscle and flesh. Blood sprayed the corpse's face as chunks of human meat fell from his mouth. He threw her body forcefully behind him into the corner of a pew. The man in black laughed at the sight.

The corpse was hungry and wasn't stopping until he got to everyone. One man ran from the door and tried to break through the blacked-out windows. The glass wouldn't break. By the time he realized the obvious truth of it, the corpse had grabbed the top of his head. The corpse dug its fingers into the man's scalp, turning his head all the way around. When that man was

mutilated enough, the corpse shoved him to the floor. Then, it leaned down and chewed on his throat while repeatedly punching into the man's stomach, pulling entrails out with every hit.

By the end of the massacre, the room was full of mutilated bodies. Blood covered the walls, and a living corpse feasted on the remains of the last to die. The man in black blinked, and the windows became normal. The lights no longer dripped blood, and the room was once again lit by the white lights. The bodies remained, however, strung about everywhere.

The man in black walked around the room, smiling at the sight of the massacre. He glanced at the corpse as it chewed on the man by the window. The sounds of it eating made him want to puke, but instead, he laughed harder.

"Looks like we're done here."

The stranger snapped his fingers. The corpse looked up and slumped over, human remains dangling from its mouth. The man stood in the middle of the room and wondered if he should make the bodies and the human-eating corpse disappear. Still grinning, he shook his head and grabbed a smoke from his pocket. It lit on its own as it had done many times before.

The man in black walked toward the double doors, kicking bodies and puddles of what used to be people out of his way. He turned and looked back at the slumped-over corpse of Thomas Jenkins by the window and snapped his fingers. The reanimated corpse sat back up and resumed chewing the flesh in its mouth.

The double doors opened, and the man walked through and exited the building. As he was about to leave the parking lot, he heard a loud crash from the funeral home. The corpse of Thomas Jenkins was crawling out of the building through a broken window onto the grass.

The stranger took a long drag from his cigarette and walked the other way.

THE END? NOT YET...

BAD TIMES AT MAX'S BAR

Max's Bar and Grill was everyone's favorite place to get a drink after work. As a matter of fact, it was the *only* place in town for anyone to grab a drink. The competition had been shut down for quite some time due to health code violations involving insects and rodents.

The owner of Max's was not named Max. His name was Todd Rivers. His father was Max, and he'd been dead a while, leaving the business to his son. When Todd took over the bar, he immediately sunk his teeth into it. He spent a lot of time and money fixing the place and ensuring everything was up to code. His father Hadn't been much on keeping things as clean as they needed to be.

One particular day, things started much as they usually did. Todd showed up at the bar around noon and started getting things ready for customers to show up around one. He made sure the bar top and the tabletops were all wiped off and the floor had been swept thoroughly.

Todd was taking the last trash bag out the back door when his main bartender, Stephanie, showed up for her shift. She through the back with her eyes glued to her cell phone. Somehow, she manoeuvred without stumbling or colliding with anything in her path.

"How do you walk without falling your face?" Todd asked Jokingly.

"Whatcha ya' mean?" she asked, looking confused.

"I mean, how do you keep your eyes on that screen and walk at the same time without falling on your ass?" He reiterated his question.

Stephanie looked up from her phone, smiled, and replied. "Pure talent, boss."

They both shared a chuckle before walking into the bar. Stephanie walked behind the bar and started making a checklist of what she needed to grab from the back cooler and pantry.

"Hey, Todd?" Stephanie hollered.

Todd came from the back, holding a clipboard. "What's wrong now, Stephanie?" he asked, smiling.

"Are we still out of the Crown Royal Apple?" she asked while checking under the bar.

"Yep. The truck won't be here for another couple of days. Why?"

"Well, that's Ol' Bill's drink of choice. You know how he gets when he doesn't get his Crown Apple and Mountain Dew." Stephanie chuckled as she marked an X over the drink in question.

"Don't think Ol' Bill will be around this evening. He mentioned last night that he was going to a funeral and was probably going fishin' after," Todd replied.

"Oh, well, that's never good. Who died?" she asked as she lit a cigarette and leaned against the bar.

"Thomas Jenkins."

"The old rich guy that owned just about everything in town?" She asked.

Todd nodded. "Yep. He didn't just own a few things in this town. Shit, he owned this town." Todd sat his clipboard on the bar top. " I think Alyssa was supposed to attend that as well.

Makes me wonder."

"What's it make you wonder?" she asked, flicking her ashes into one of the bar top ashtrays.

"Well, I had a long talk with that girl the other night about her damn drug use. She has shown up for her last three shifts all fucked up. Told her if she comes in like that again, she's gone. But what I'm wondering is, why would Alyssa be going to Thomas Jenkins' funeral? I never saw them together."

"I am pretty sure I've seen her wait on him a bunch. Probably just a good tipper." Stephanie quickly replied.

"Yeah, maybe." Todd combed his gray hair with his left hand. "Or maybe there was something else going on."

"Oh, Toddy! You always are a curious one, aren't you?" She joked.

"What can I say? I like a good mystery." Todd cracked a grin and headed to his office in the back while Stephanie finished gathering beers for the coolers under the bar.

When it was time to switch the CLOSED side of the sign to the OPEN side, there were already five people waiting to come in—the usual crowd that came in before anyone else, the old-timers. These were people who had come in at the same time for many, many years. They all knew Max when he ran the place, and they had always told him they would stay loyal until the time came that they were no longer around.

"Hey, sweetheart. You care to turn that television on for me?" An elderly gentleman asked Stephanie.

Stephanie smiled. "For you, Eugene, of course!" Stephanie reached up above the bar and

flipped the TV on. It was an older set that still had some life left in it. Todd had been saying he would replace all the sets in the building with flat screens. The time had not come yet. It would probably be a while before it did.

As soon as the television was on, there was a breaking news report. A female news anchor spoke:

"Police have stated no one has any information on the tragedy at the funeral home. It's also being reported that the body of the deceased, Thomas Jenkins, is missing. Police received the call this morning shortly after Ten A.M." As the news anchor kept talking, everyone in the bar watched attentively. While the anchor spoke, the screen flipped back and forth between footage of the funeral home and body bags being carried out. "The person who made the call said they would rather not be known, just that they had arrived for a different wake and funeral scheduled for later in the day."

The bar became quieter. Everyone was in shock, seeing what was being reported.

Todd came out of his office just in time to overhear TV. "Holy shit!" He shouted.

Everyone in the bar turned to look at him.

"Todd, wasn't that the funeral Bill Fisher and Alyssa were supposed to be at today?" Stephanie asked with a tone of concern.

Todd stood at the end of the bar with his hand covering his mouth and a look of shock on his face. "Yeah, that's the one." He grabbed a bottled beer from the cooler behind the bar, chugging it down within seconds of opening it.

"You okay?" Stephanie asked.

Todd gave her a look, not saying anything. He grabbed a bottle of whiskey and filled up a shot glass. The shot disappeared quicker than the beer. Slamming the shot glass on the bar, he turned to Stephanie. "This is horrible."

Todd was never the rough and tough guy like his father. His anger rarely got the best of him. He was a caring person, and even if he had issues with certain people, he never wanted to see anyone getting hurt.

"Pretty insane, isn't it?" an old woman sitting at the bar sipping a vodka and Sprite chimed in.

Todd turned and looked at the woman. "Yeah, definitely."

A large bearded man, probably in his early thirties, burst through the door. He was pouring sweat. "They're dead! Did you see the news?" he shouted as he sat on one of the bar stools. His name was Ned Fisher, the brother of Ol' Bill, who had attended the wake.

"Yeah, we just finished watching it. It didn't say anything about who all was dead." Stephanie replied.

Ned looked at Stephanie with tears rolling down his face. "The cops called our mom and let us know. They're not releasing it to the public yet."

Stephanie poured a double shot of cheap whiskey and placed the glass in front of Ned. Without skipping a beat, he gulped it down. Stephanie poured him another. He took that one with lightning speed, as well.

"Ned, I am so sorry. Billy was a good customer and a good man," Stephanie said.

"No, my brother was an asshole, but..." Ned trailed off and took another shot, "...he was my brother."

With the news report and Ned's confirmation that Billy was dead, the room became somber. Ned got drunk and played a bunch of songs on the old jukebox, crying off and on through all of them.

Stephanie was about to sneak a shot when her cell phone vibrated in her back pocket. She reached behind her and grabbed her phone. The look on her face at what she read alarmed a few people who were sitting near her. Todd ran from the back before Stephanie could say anything to anyone.

"I just got a text!" Todd said.

"I did, too. Alyssa is dead," she replied.

"Yeah, that's the text I got, too." The news visibly shook Todd.

"Goddammit! Alyssa is dead, too?" Ned shouted, overhearing the conversation.

"Who messaged you about it?" Stephanie asked curiously.

"A cop friend of mine. He just found out the names of the people who died and knew Alyssa worked for me. Who told you about it?" Todd inquired.

"One of my girlfriends. Her brother works for the newspaper," Stephanie answered, pouring another shot for Ned and one for Todd.

"Go ahead and pour yourself one, also. I know you need one," Todd insisted.

Another hour passed, and a few more people entered the bar. Everyone turned to look at an unfamiliar person who entered. The man was dressed in all black, and his hair was dark and slicked back. He took a seat at the bar.

"What can I get for ya?" Stephanie asked the stranger as she walked to where he sat.

The man looked at her and grinned. "I think I would like to have..." He glanced at the choices behind the bar. "...that one in the black bottle! That looks like a winner!" The man's voice was chipper and raspy, while his eyes were unnerving and dark—almost black.

As Stephanie poured a shot for the stranger, Ned drunkenly rushed over and sat beside the man.

"Buddy, you don't look to be from around here. Why are you here?" Ned's words worried Stephanie. The last thing she wanted was trouble. Ned was in the right mood, not to mention drunk enough, to want to start shit with someone.

"Ned! I know it's been a horrible day for you, but I can't have you being a drunk asshole to customers!" Stephanie snapped.

The stranger smiled and waved as Ned walked back to his seat. The man pulled a cigarette from his breast pocket and put it in his mouth.

Stephanie pulled her lighter from her pocket, raising it to the man's unlit cigarette, and gave it a flick. A small flame came out of the lighter. The man took a healthy drag and exhaled a large cloud of smoke, almost resembling a skull.

"So, I am sorry for Ned over there and how he acted, but I am kind of curious myself about who you are. This being a small town, everyone here knows everyone, and we don't know you." Stephanie politely enquired.

The man grinned and took another puff off his cigarette. He leaned in, teeth biting down on the cigarette, grinning from ear to ear, and smoke coming out of his nose. "You really wanna know why I am here?" He asked.

Stephanie couldn't help it. She was a tad nervous to know the answer but nodded anyway.

The man's voice went low, and his grin faded. "Well, not that it's really anyone's business..." He stopped and looked around to see who was listening. Everyone at the bar seemed to be paying attention. "I'm supposed to be meeting up with someone here." He exhaled a cloud of smoke from his nose and let out a raspy laugh.

Stephanie looked frightened.

"No need to be worried. I was just fucking with you. Why does everyone seem so on edge in here?" He smirked.

"Well, to be honest, our little community went through a pretty bad tragedy earlier today. Ned happens to be the brother of one of the victims. One of our waitresses was also killed," She replied, lighting a cigarette of her own.

"Sounds like a tragedy, indeed. What happened?" The man asked, squinting as if he looked forward to hearing her answer.

"Honestly, no one knows. A bunch of people were found at a funeral home, slaughtered. It happened during the wake service." She took a drag off her cigarette and exhaled.

"Wow! That does sound like some kind of tragic mystery," he replied, sporting a half-cocked grin.

"Yeah. The body of the man whose service it was disappeared."

"Now, that is something. Where do you think a corpse would walk off to?" the man in black joked.

"Mister, I don't think that's a funny thing to say! Poor Ned over there has been a mess since he found out!" Stephanie snapped, offended by his comments.

The stranger put his hands in front of him. "Hey, I'm sorry. Sometimes, I make jokes that many don't find too funny. My apologies, ma'am." He put his cigarette out in the ashtray. "With that said, could I get that bottle of whatever you just poured me, please? I really enjoyed that stuff."

"The whole bottle? I think it may be the only one we have left," Stephanie replied.

The stranger put his hand in his pocket, pulled out a wad of cash, and threw down a one-hundred-dollar bill. "That's for the bottle." He slapped down another hundred-dollar bill next to the first one. "And here's a little something for you."

"Well, I mean, yeah. I guess if you're gonna put that much down for it... Don't see why it would hurt." Stephanie's mood lifted slightly when she saw the money. However, this made her more concerned about the mystery man and his intentions. There was something creepy yet intriguing about him. She quickly grabbed the bottle and a tall glass and sat them on the bar top in front of the man, flashing him a little grin.

"Much obliged," said the stranger as he poured the brown liquor into his glass, almost to the point of overflowing. "Bottoms up!" he enthusiastically announced. With everyone watching, he downed the whiskey like water and immediately filled the glass again, slamming it down. "Stuff is delightful," he muttered.

Todd came walking up from the back to talk to Stephanie when he noticed the strange gentleman guzzling whiskey at the bar.

"Who's the weird-looking dude? You know him?" Todd whispered into Stephanie's ear.

"Nope," she whispered back. "He came in about twenty minutes ago. Said he's meeting someone here."

Todd scratched his head. "Okay, well, keep an eye on him. With that weird shit going on this morning, I don't want to take any chances."

"Aye aye, boss," Stephanie replied, still in a whisper.

It was three o'clock, and the stranger was still sitting at the bar top, alone. He'd finished the bottle he'd bought an hour before. Everyone kept watching him and whispering about him while he sat there contently chain-smoking. It didn't seem to bother him. He was keeping busy with a small notebook.

Stephanie began wiping puddles and smudges off the bar. As she neared the man, she spoke up. "So, what time is your friend coming to meet you?"

The man looked up from his notebook and grinned. "Oh, it's not a friend." He chuckled. "No, I'm not sure when this person will be here. I just know they will come in this bar at some point, and I must be waiting for them."

His answer wasn't what Stephanie expected. Her mind was racing. Her first thought was he might be some kind of bounty hunter or, even worse, a hitman. Giving the man a quick grin, she walked around the bar and went back to Todd's office.

"Hey, boss."

Startled, he raised his head from his papers. "Stephanie! What are you doing back here? Is that weirdo gone yet?"

"No. He's still up there. Still no sign of the person he's here to meet with."

"Then why are you back here? I told you to watch that guy!" Todd verged on hysteria as he was prone to when a situation caused him any amount of stress.

"Well, I need to talk to you. I'm getting a weird feeling. Like, this guy may be looking to do bad to whoever he's meeting with." Stephanie peered out the door and saw the stranger sitting at the bar. She walked back to Todd's desk.

"Yeah? What makes you think that?" he asked, wiping the sweat from his brow with a handkerchief.

"Just the things he was saying. Something does not seem right."

Todd sighed. "Well, until there's any real proof of him planning to do harm, just keep an eye on him. The first sign of trouble, you tell me, and we'll stop it before it starts—whatever it may be." He looked down at the papers on his desk, not wanting to make eye contact with Stephanie. "Now, go out there and be a good spy." He tried to laugh but worried his young employee was correct. Something terrible was going to happen.

Stephanie returned to the bar and resumed her usual duties of keeping the bar clean and the glasses filled. A couple sitting at a booth near the front door had just left. She noticed they hadn't thrown away any of their bottles or trash. They had left her a decent tip, so she wasn't too salty about it. As she cleaned the booth, two people walked through the door.

"Welcome to Max's, guys! Pick anywhere you would like to sit, and I will be with you in just a minute," She announced as she tossed empty bottles into the trash can. She glanced at the stranger, who seemed to take notice of the men sitting down at a round, high-top table about five or six feet away from him at the bar.

"Okay, sorry. I had to clean up someone's mess," Stephanie said playfully to the men.

"That's mighty alright, miss. I'll just have a Coors," one of the men said. He wore a backward cap on his head and sported a shirt with the word WINNER on the front.

"And for you?" she asked the second man.

"Think I'll have me a Coors, too, and a double shot of whatever cheap whiskey you got back there," The second man said hastily.

Both men were from that area, but Stephanie couldn't remember their names. She was pretty sure that the one wearing the WINNER shirt had been arrested at some point for robbery a few years back. She couldn't place the other guy at all. He just fit the description of what she envisioned as a nothing-but-trouble kind of guy.

The stranger at the bar leaned back on his bar stool, listening to everything he could that was being said between the two men. As he did, he took notes in his notebook.

"Okay, dude! Why the fuck are we here?" The WINNER guy asked his friend.

"I don't know. I figured we'd stop here and have a drink. Got a long journey ahead of us. Might be what we need," said the other guy as he scratched a sore on his neck.

"What is up with your neck? You've been fucking with it since you picked me up." The WINNER guy looked disgusted as he spoke.

"Don't know. Not worried about it. The goddamn thing is itchy as fuck, though. It's probably just some bug bite. It is summer. They're everywhere," he said, laughing.

Stephanie hurried to the office again.

Todd quickly grabbed a stack of papers to cover his lap. The poor bastard had a problem with chronic masturbation when he got nervous. While he figured he had a minute, he'd opened an old Hustler magazine, found a spread of two women in the sixty-nine position, and went to town on himself, thinking he would be done before any more interruptions occurred. Of course, he should have known better, but he was in luck. It didn't seem like Stephanie had seen anything when she barged in. He was, however, concerned that if the papers covering his penis were to fall on the floor, there wouldn't be much left for Stephanie's imagination.

"I think something is up."

"For fuck's sake, kid! You watch too many movies or something!" he said, acting as if he weren't using the papers on his lap to cover himself. "What do you mean? Is someone talkin' shit or something? I have a lot on my plate right now." he said, looking up from the mess of papers.

"No, but I am pretty sure the guy... that one guy was waiting on just came in. He didn't say anything to him, but he's been paying a lot of attention to two guys who just came in. He hasn't paid any attention to anyone else until these guys showed up."

The worry in Stephanie's voice and the way she bit her lip didn't ease Todd's concern about the current situation in his establishment. "Think he is going to try something?" he asked.

"Surely, if he were, he wouldn't do it in here with everyone watching. Would he?" she asked, almost grinding her bottom lip.

"Steph, you never know. Weirdo fucks like that guy are unpredictable." Though put on a joking tone, he was not joking at all. As he considered what he was being told, he was beyond serious.

"What should we—"

Before Stephanie could finish her sentence, a blood-curdling scream came from the front of the building. She and Todd ran to the bar. One of the older women had fainted. Todd ran to her.

"Oh my god," Todd muttered under his breath.

Frozen with fear, everyone focused on the round table. Stephanie started shaking and felt like she was going to piss herself.

"What the hell is that thing?" A man sitting at the end of the bar shouted.

Where the two men had been sitting, one of the men now stood in front of the table. The wound on his neck had opened and was getting bigger and nastier. What appeared to be a long, blackish-green, slimy arm extended from his neck, digging into the WINNER guy's stomach. Vile, wet sounds filled the air as the mutated man's extra appendage dug around in the other man's insides, squeezing intestines until they burst. Little by little, loose innards started dangling from the WINNER guy's body. Every time something fell from his gut, it made a SPLAT on the floor, as did the sound of bar patrons vomiting—SPLAT! SPLAT! SPLAT!—all over the bar floor.

The man with the creature coming from his neck looked frozen, like whatever was inside him was taking him over. A strange gurgling came from inside his gut. The man wearing the now ripped-apart WINNER shirt just stood there while this thing played with his insides like playdough. He looked like he was in shock. The creature's arm, still protruding from the other guy's neck, broke through WINNER guy's ribs, crushing his chest plate and grabbing his heart, giving it a good squeeze. The WINNER guy sank to his knees and fell backward onto the concrete floor. The creature's arm slid out as he fell. Blood and chunks of innards dripped from its long fingers and rigid nails.

Stephanie took her eyes off the mess and looked around for the strange man dressed in black. He was no longer where he'd been sitting in the whole time.

"Where the fuck did he go?" she asked herself.

She looked at every angle of the bar and didn't see him until she looked at the front door. There he was, standing against the front door in the darkness. His black attire made it easy for him to blend into the shadows. She ran to the opposite side of the bar, hurrying over to him.

"What the hell is going on?" she frantically asked him.

The man was placing a cigarette into his mouth when he grinned at her.

"I watched you paying attention to those men when they came in. You didn't give two shits about anyone else! Is this who you were waiting for?" Stephanie shouted.

"My dear, you are correct," he replied.

"Then what is going on? Were you about to leave without stopping this?" she frantically asked as they looked back at the man standing at the round table. He was slowly being ripped open, this time from his gut.

The man turned to look Stephanie in the face. She watched as the cigarette in his mouth lit itself. Her eyes widened at the sight.

"Now, why would I do that? Stop it? Hell, woman! I was here to make sure he showed up and did his job!" The man in black took a big inhale from his cigarette and blew the smoke directly into Stephanie's shocked face. "Now, I gotta get going, little lady. But, if I were you, I would think of something. When that thing over there finally rips through that guy, he's gonna kill everyone in this bar." He kicked the door open and walked outside, whistling happily as he went.

"Wait! What are we supposed to do?" Stephanie hollered, trying to get outside to catch him, but he was already gone.

"We gotta get out of here!" Ned screamed. He ran to the front door and pushed Stephanie out of the way. However, it did no good. The door slammed in his face as he tried to exit the building. "You fucking sonofabitch!" He pulled a small caliber pistol from his jacket and started firing at the creature. It was no use. The thing wasn't phased by a single bullet that hit it.

A loud ROAR and more gurgling came from inside the body the creature inhabited. The sound of ripping flesh and bones breaking accompanied the creature's fast rate of growth. The creature's arm retracted like a tape measure back inside the body before bursting out of the chest area. More limbs sprouted from the new opening. When both arms were through the chest hole, they reached down and ripped off the man's legs one by one. Long, greenish-gray legs pushed through the open thigh sockets. The man's lifeless head wiggled as something ate its way out from the inside of his neck.

Everyone stood in horror, watching as the creature's head finally appeared. The misshapen cranium poked from the vacant area between the man's shoulders. It tore the rest of the human cocoon off with its sharp claws and threw it against the wall with a wet SPLAT! The tall, ugly motherfucker stood amidst the piles of gore littering the floor. Its large teeth were sharp and rigid. A red and green slime covered its body.

"Goddamn you!" Ned cried out as he drunkenly ran to attack the creature.

"Ned, DON'T!" Stephanie hollered.

Ned didn't listen. By the time Stephanie yelled for him, it was already too late. The creature grabbed Ned by the top of his head, twisting it around. Ned didn't have time to scream. His arms fell to his sides. The creature twisted until his spine cracked and his head dislocated from his neck. It dug its claws into the skull, pulling upward with aggressive force. Ned's body fell when the flesh keeping his neck intact snapped. The creature snarled, holding Ned's head—appraising it. It spoke in a gurgled voice, "Ned...tasty!"

Its mouth opened wider, showing an extra set of smaller teeth surrounding the inside. The remaining people in the room were too frightened to move. Frozen by fear, they watched in disgust as the creature devoured Ned's severed head. It bit down with its grotesque teeth, crunching particles of bone between its jaws as it chewed. Ned's eyeballs popped from their sockets, busting against the rigid points. With one final bite and swallow, Ned's head was gone.

The creature stood in the middle of the bar, looking at the mess it had made. Seeing the scared expressions on the faces of the bar patrons seemed to amuse the creature. A sound almost resembling a jumbled laugh came from its throat.

People scattered. One man tried to open the front door, but it wouldn't budge. Others ran to the bathrooms to hide. Stephanie ran to see if the back door would open. Todd, who had the same idea, was at the back door trying to break it down—it was useless.

"Why won't this damn thing open? We're going to die!" Todd said frantically. Stephanie grabbed her boss by both shoulders and looked him in the eye.

"No, we're not! There must be some way to get out of here." She wanted to believe her own words, but she didn't. Everything happening that day was bad after bad. Nothing pointed to a happy ending, but she knew she needed to keep trying to figure something out. Giving up was not an option.

"The doors won't open..." Todd paused. "The windows!" Todd ran back into the front room. He ran past the creature, quickly grabbed a bar stool, and chucked it at one of the big windows. The stool bounced off. "Shit!" He shouted.

"Todd! Get back here!" Stephanie hollered.

She poked her head out of the back office and realized her hollering caught the creature's ear. It turned around, looking her straight in the eye, and started walking toward her. She backed into the office and slammed the door.

"Stephanie! Grab the pistol from my desk!" Todd yelled from the front room.

Stephanie pushed a bunch of shelves in front of the door, barricading it the best she could. She rifled through the desk, throwing papers all over the place.

"Dammit, Todd! Where do you keep that thing?" She noticed one place she hadn't looked. Under the desk was a small lock box that she knew Todd never locked. She opened it up and found a small caliber pistol.

After grabbing the pistol, Stephanie couldn't hear anything. Silence... She didn't hear screaming, yelling, or anything from upfront. She kicked the desk and the rest of the barricade out from in front of the door.

The door creaked as she slowly cracked it open. There wasn't anyone in sight. Upon opening the door some more, the coast seemed clear. She ventured out into the hallway.

"STEPHANIE!" Todd came out of nowhere, making her jump—causing her to squeeze the pistol's trigger. The barrel was pointed downward. The round went into Todd's foot, dropping him to the ground. "MOTHERFUCKER!" He cried out.

"Shit! I am so sorry! You scared me!" She leaned down to console Todd, checking how badly he was hurt.

"It's fine. Hurts like a sonofabitch, but I think I'll live," he replied as he got back up on his feet. "That thing disappeared. I have no idea where it went either!"

"Think it left?" She asked.

Todd scratched his forehead. "I don't know. Maybe."

They walked up to the front of the bar. It was a mess. Blood splattered on the walls and ceiling. Strands of flesh were strung about like garland. There was no sign of the creature,

however. Todd walked behind the bar, grabbed a tall glass, and poured himself a brew from the tap. He sighed, then chugged the entire glass, belching loudly when it was empty.

Stephanie walked up behind him and tapped him on the shoulder. "Don't be leaving me out, old man. I've had a long couple of hours, just like you," Stephanie joked.

Todd handed her a glass. Stephanie poured herself a beer, almost overflowing the pint glass. She gulped the whole glass down faster than Todd had chugged his.

"Always have to one-up me on everything, don't ya'?" Todd said, shaking his head, unable to wrap his mind around what was happening.

CRASH!

"What the hell was that?" Stephanie looked at Todd, startled.

The loud crash came from behind him in the hallway leading to the office. The creature had crashed through the ceiling. Todd and Stephanie jumped back. They both knew that letting their guard down, thinking the creature was gone, had been a mistake. Together, they turned to look down the hallway.

The creature was hunched over, inhaling aggressively.

"Goddamn you!" Todd screamed at it.

A chuckle-like sound gargled from the creature's throat.

Todd grabbed an aluminum baseball bat from behind the bar. Attempting to rush the creature, he limped forward, raising the bat high, hoping to slam it down on its skull. The creature flung its long, scaly arm out and knocked Todd against the wall. His body smacked so hard it cracked the drywall.

Stephanie almost forgot about the pistol. She pulled the firearm from the back of her

pants. Without thinking, she rushed to the creature and pointed the barrel at its head.

Another wet chuckle erupted from its throat.

"Laugh at this, you ugly motherfucker!"

She squeezed the trigger over and over, emptying the cylinder into the creature's face. With every shot, thick, greenish-crimson ooze splashed out. The creature's laugh changed to an agonized wail. It fell to its knees and sadly looked up at Stephanie. Stephanie knew better than to feel any sympathy for that thing.

From down by her knees, it continued to look up at her. Stephanie was about to start bashing its head in with the empty gun when the back door blasted open. Stephanie leaned forward and saw the man from earlier—the man in black—standing in the hallway holding a double-barrel shotgun.

"WHO THE FUCK ARE YOU?" Stephanie shouted, sounding exhausted.

With a big, shit-eating grin, the man in black walked over to where Stephanie stood with the creature at her feet. He looked down at the abomination and pointed the double barrel at its head, pressing the muzzle hard into its scalp.

"I have never dealt with such a useless piece of shit before." He paused, looked at Stephanie, and grinned. "And I deal with plenty of humans." He squeezed both triggers.

KA-PLOW!

Both barrels were released into the creature's already fucked up head. The blast finished the job Stephanie had started. The rest of its hideous head exploded. Chunks of mutant flesh, shards of teeth, and brain matter blanketed the room. Blood and innards dripped from the dangling light fixture, casting an eerie glow.

Stephanie stood there in a state of disbelief. Her face and body were covered in goo. The man in black was covered in viscera as well.

The man in black threw the shotgun on the ground and placed a cigarette between his lips. The cigarette lit on its own. He smiled. "Man, you look like shit," He commented to a perplexed Stephanie.

Stephanie scowled at the man and got in his face. "What is so fucking funny, you lunatic? What are you? Why are you here?" she questioned, screaming in his face.

The man took a drag from his cigarette and blew the smoke in her face. "Honey, there would be zero point in explaining who and what I am and why I am here."

Stephanie backed up. "Why did you bring that thing here?"

"Oh, I didn't bring him. He was already here. It's my job to make sure of certain things when it comes to the escaped ones," the man in black said calmly. "I was simply making sure he fulfilled his duties. Clearly, he did not."

"MOTHERFUCKER!" Todd screamed as he got up from where he'd been knocked and charged at the man in black.

"Oh, I wouldn't do that," the man in black advised, holding his hand out in front of him.

"Don't hurt him!" Stephanie cried out.

With his arm still held out, the man in black made a fist. This motion seemed to cause Todd to fall face forward on the wood floor. His face smacked so hard that his front teeth broke off with the impact. "Didn't say I wouldn't hurt him, but he's not dead."

Stephanie sighed before running to Todd's aid. He was face down on the floor. When he raised his head, blood spilled from his mouth and nose. Before Todd could say anything, a ruckus

sounded outside the bar.

Stephanie and Todd were silent. The man in black walked over to them and put his hand out to Todd. Todd grabbed his hand back. With a tough pull, Todd was back on his feet. Stephanie lifted herself back up from the floor.

"Sorry about that, friend. Losing a few teeth is better than what I could have done," The man in black said as all three of them walked to the window to see what was going on outside.

"What the hell?" Todd mumbled as he looked out the window.

Walking around in front of the bar was a man. His clothes had been cut off in the back and were about to fall off. His flesh looked gray, and his face was covered in a red substance.

"Is that Thomas Jenkins?" Todd ran to a different window for a better look. "Holy shit!"

"Yeah. That's him." The man in black poked his head between Todd and Stephanie's heads. They both looked at him, confused. "That poor son of a bitch had it all. He chose to use his power for selfish pleasure and evil deeds. What you are looking at is a man who is damned—a member of the undead, if you will. You can call him a zombie or a flesh eater. But you want to know what he really is? A shitbag with legs."

"Are you kidding me?" Todd asked.

"You can see, right?" The man in black smirked.

Todd flared his nostrils. "No reason to be a smart-ass," he said under his breath.

"Then there's no reason to question me."

"But why?" Stephanie asked as she watched Thomas Jenkins' dead ass stumble down the gravel parking lot, heading towards the fields across the road.

The man in black scratched his brow, smirking as his eyes met hers. "Can't say." He put

another cigarette in his mouth. Once again, it lit itself.

Todd and Stephanie glanced at each other, wanting to comment, but saw no reason.

"I will say that I think I could use a drink." He pulled out a fifty-dollar bill followed by a crisp one-hundred-dollar bill. "Shit, you all look like you could use one or three drinks, too." He chuckled as they all walked to the bar.

The man in black sat back in the seat he'd used earlier. Todd sat beside him. Stephanie went behind the bar and grabbed an expensive bottle of whiskey and three glasses. Sitting next to Todd at the bar, she poured the drinks to the rim. They sat in silence, sipping their drinks.

The man in black chuckled to himself. Todd and Stephanie weren't as pleased. Both were in their own heads, looking for the answers to what the fuck was going on. Had they really been witness to all that? The last question they both asked themselves was an important one: *How much worse will things get?*

Outside, a very angry, naked, and bloodthirsty corpse found itself creeping through the trees, occasionally coming up on a house or two. It punched out the windows of parked cars and threw trash cans into homes, leaving a trail of glass as it continued its journey to nowhere. It made awful chewing sounds as leftover chunks of skin fell from the back of its mouth to its front teeth. Its jaws clamped together, making squishy sounds every time it gnashed its teeth.

Being that the corpse was no longer Thomas Jenkins, just a walking, oozing shell of what was once a man, It had no concept of time or distance. Its legs had been walking, more like dragging, for about an hour until it wandered through an open section of fence. The sounds of multiple voices up ahead reminded the corpse of its mission to keep eating.

NO POINT IN SAYING THE END JUST YET...

DEAD CROP

The sun was going down, and the heat from the long, hot day was cooling off. For most people living out in the country, it was the time of day to sit on the front porch, alone or with someone special, to sip whiskey and drink beer. However, that evening was not so relaxing for brothers Danny and Zeke Whitaker.

"I swear! We will have it all in three days. It won't be a problem. I promise!" Zeke was on the phone with the man they called their boss. He wasn't very nice at times and, frankly, scared the hell out of both brothers.

"Who the hell was that?" Danny asked as he walked into the kitchen.

Zeke took a deep breath and pushed END on his cell phone. "Who do you think it was?" He looked up at Danny.

"Shit, Zeke! Was that Clayton?"

"Bingo," Zeke replied, reaching for his beer on the counter.

"I told you, man! We shouldn't have sold those plants! Those weren't ours to sell! That man is going to hang us by our toes and have wild boars chewing on our heads!" Danny said, spitting a huge wad of chewed-up chewing tobacco.

Zeke slowly glanced at his brother again, shaking his head. "What is wrong with you?"

"What?" Danny replied.

"You're crazy. Clayton isn't going to do that to us. We'll get everything taken care of and be back on track." Zeke was always pretty sure of himself. He'd gotten them out of many tricky situations before—but this was a big one.

"I hope you're right." Danny's words didn't sound very convincing. However, deep down, he felt his brother would save the day once again. What worried him was the idea that luck could run out at any time; this was what concerned him most.

"Look, don't worry. Go into the living room and grab the tray. I'll role us a fat boy to smoke, and I'll pour some shots of the good stuff!" Zeke knew weed and alcohol were pretty good ways to get his younger brother to chill out.

"Fine." Danny sounded like a child who didn't get his way. But with weed and booze, he was definitely getting his way.

The two sat at the kitchen table, smoking a joint the size of their thumbs and discussing what they were going to do to save their asses. Zeke took three big drags off the joint, which had been lit for a minute by that point.

"Okay, so here is what we are gonna do." Zeke's hands were out in front of him, moving as he talked. With his voice and body language, he could pass for a car salesman. "I messaged an old friend of mine earlier. He agreed to help us." He took a swig of the beer in front of him. "He's going to front us a couple of plants and a few ounces of bud to cover what we sold of Clayton's. He's giving us a few weeks to pay him back. After we get everything we owe back to Clayton and get our cut, we will be golden on paying Shane back!" Zeke took another hit from the joint and passed it to Danny.

"Not a bad plan...ummm...who's Shane?" Danny asked with eyes of red.

"Shane's the guy who is fronting us the weed!" Zeke shook his head and laughed. "You sure you need to smoke that?"

Danny took a long drag from the joint and almost immediately started to hack from the smoke. "Yeah," he coughed. "I'm good." He started a coughing fit that lasted almost three minutes.

Zeke chuckled and stood up from the table. "You sound like you need a beer, my brother!"

Because coughing made speaking difficult, Danny just nodded, YES.

Zeke peered into the fridge. The following statement he uttered was simple and depressing. "No beer." He closed the fridge and sat back down at the table, looking bummed.

"Wait!" Danny hollered out, giving one last harsh cough. "Man, there is a whole case of coldies down at the Hut!"

"Shit, I forgot about those! Let's go get 'em!" Zeke hollered as both men ran for their boots by the back door.

***

The Hut was the name of the building they kept near their outdoor marijuana plants. They used the building as a place to hang freshly picked buds to dry and to trim the leaves off the buds. It wasn't a huge place, but it had a decent living room and a working toilet. Often, the two would get too drunk and stoned working at night to walk back up to their house. So, they made sure to keep plenty of beer down at the Hut.

"Man, that damn walk about kills me anymore," Danny complained.

"Yeah, it kinda' sucks, doesn't it?" Zeke replied, grunting as he walked through the darkening woods. "Glad it's not much further."

"Yeah, no shit! But I can almost taste the cold beer now! "Danny replied, smacking his lips like he was dying of thirst.

Finally making it through the woods and down the hill, reaching the Hut, they quickly ran to the door and unlocked it. As soon as they were inside, Zeke flipped the light switch. The room was filled with an array of cannabis hanging from the ceiling and two tables with a few buds on them. Multiple baskets, usually full of buds, were lying on the floor. A shower curtain in the corner hid a toilet. Two refrigerators sat on the opposite side of the room.

"Hell yeah!" Both mini-fridges are full!" Danny gleefully shouted, picking up a couple of plastic grocery bags from a pile beside the fridges. He began filling them with cans of beer.

Zeke walked to a window that was paneled over with plywood and opened a little spy hole he'd built in. He peered out at all the plants growing in their field. He couldn't help wishing the strain of cannabis their boss needed was among them. He'd thought about trying to play off the whole thing by handing over plants and saying they were the strain he needed. Deep down, he knew that if that plan didn't work, he and his brother would end up like Danny said—boar food.

"Hey, Zeke! Care to give me a hand here?" Danny was trying to fill his arms with cans of beer while holding the two full bags.

"Shit! Yeah, Dan! My bad." As Zeke was about to leave the peephole to help his brother,

he turned, glancing back out one last time. He did a double take—something strange caught his eye.

"Zeke! A little help here?" Beers were about to fall from Danny's arms.

"Dude, there is someone out there!"

Danny could tell Zeke wasn't kidding around by the tone of his voice. The thought that the cops might be about to raid sent a pang of fear through his guts. "What do you mean there's someone out there?"

Danny walked to the window, his arms full of cans. Zeke moved over so he could look.

"Holy shit! Who the fuck is that?" Danny could see the silhouette of someone sauntering through some of the almost fully grown plants. "What do we do?"

"You know what we have to do," Zeke sighed. He reached to the back of his jeans and pulled out a small-caliber pistol with six in the cylinder. "We gotta go get them off this property of ours!"

After Danny set his cans down on the floor, the brothers walked out the door toward the field of cannabis plants. They made their way around The Hut to find a man standing there. He was naked and stumbling around as if drunk.

"What the..." Danny reacted.

Zeke pointed the pistol in the direction of the naked man. "Hey, Fucko! You are in the wrong place to be prancing along in the woods!" He expected the man to turn the other way, or get down on his knees and beg for his life, or put his hands up—something... But there was no reaction of the sort.

The man made a hissing noise.

"Why is this guy not acting scared, Zeke?"

"I have no idea, little brother," Zeke replied.

"Hey, man! We will shoot your ass if you don't answer us!" Danny shouted at the naked trespasser.

The man stood there staring at the brothers.

Zeke walked closer to him, cocking the pistol's hammer back. "I am going to say this once! Put your hands up and tell us why you are here!"

The naked man didn't put his hands up. He just started walking toward them. As he moved, he stepped into a beam of moonlight. Even in the dim light, the brothers were shocked by what they saw.

The naked man looked like he was rotting. His flesh looked gray or green—maybe a mixture of both. Blood covered his face and body.

"Is this a fucking zombie?" Danny asked nervously.

"A zombie? No! That's stupid..." Zeke trailed off, questioning his own reply. He hollered to the man again. "Hey! Stop! Or I am going to empty this gun into you!"

The man didn't stop. As he ambled forward, he opened his mouth. His teeth were rigid.

"That's it!" Zeke opened fire.

BAM!

BAM!

BAM!

With each shot, a greenish-black substance flew out of the man's body, splashing all over the many plants surrounding him.

BAM!

BAM!

BAM!

Zeke fired the last shot into the man's head, causing it to explode on impact. The naked man flew backward. Chunks of brain and skull splattered his surroundings.

The brothers ran to where the man lay. The greenish goo that came from his wounds was everywhere.

"Goddammit! That stuff is all over our plants, man!" Danny shouted.

"I see that." Zeke knelt to get a closer look at the naked man's body. "Jesus Christ!"

"What, Zeke?" Concern was all over Danny's face.

"It's our bosses' boss!" Zeke shouted. He turned and looked at Danny.

"That Jenkins guy?"

"Yeah..." Zeke looked down at the naked man. "This doesn't make any sense..."

"Why not?" Danny asked curiously.

Zeke looked back up at Danny, biting his lip, trying not to say anything mean. "Well, it really doesn't make sense that he's running around in our weed field naked and covered in blood. It also doesn't make sense that he bled green goo when I shot him." He waited for Danny to respond. When Danny didn't, he continued. "And it really doesn't make any sense because he fucking died the other day!"

"He died?" Danny pulled a pack of chew from his back pocket. He pinched a good bit and placed it in the side of his mouth.

"Yeah, he keeled over the other day, and there was a bunch of weird shit all over the news about his body missing," Zeke replied as he stood up from kneeling. "I just thought it was some kind of weird prank or something. I really didn't think his fucking body literally got up and walked away!" No matter how he tried to look at it, there was no explanation for what was happening.

"What the fuck, Zeke? What are we going to do?"

"Not sure. This is bad. This is really bad." Zeke lowered his tone. "Jenkins and Clayton have worked together for years. If anyone finds this body here, our trouble might just double."

The brothers stood in their pot field, staring at the naked man once known as Thomas Jenkins. Danny chewed his tobacco and wondered how many of those buds got covered in the undead goo. While Zeke wondered the same thing, he also thought about the best way to get rid of the body—not to mention everything else they needed to get away with to pay Clayton back.

"We could always just chop up the body and bury it somewhere," Danny proposed.

"Yeah, there is that. But where would we be able to bury him where the dogs won't dig him up?" Zeke scratched his head.

"Burn 'em?"

"I thought of that too. The only problem—we burn a body, and it's gonna stink. Not to mention, I am not quite sure how bad this thing would smell if we did." Zeke motioned for Danny to follow him back to the building.

Walking into the Hut, both brothers immediately ran to the beers Danny had left on the floor. They each grabbed two and began chugging. Before they knew it, they'd downed a six-pack apiece and felt pretty good.

"Goddamn, I was thirsty!" Danny shouted out, letting out a chuckle in the process.

"Same! Going down smooth," Zeke replied, finishing his sixth beer.

"So... what's the plan?" Danny asked.

Zeke had been sitting in the middle of the floor, gripping a beer in each hand, taking swigs from each simultaneously. He struggled for a minute to lift himself up from where he sat. Upon successfully managing to stand, he stumbled over to the peephole in the wood-covered window. The corpse still lay among the weed plants, dripping green slime.

"When it comes to the body, I'm still thinking. When it comes to the buds, we are gonna treat them like normal. We'll dry them out and sell 'em." Zeke declared.

"We're gonna sell it?" Danny asked, shocked.

"Yep. We sure are! I don't see why not. I mean, how much damage could that stuff cause? It's fuckin' great weed—and don't people dip doobies in formaldehyde? Just gotta' dry it out like I said, bag it up, and we are good to go!" Zeke spoke with his usual confidence.

"I mean, I'm with ya' if you think it will work..."

"I do, little brother, I really do." Zeke smiled and grabbed another beer, grinning from ear to ear, not wanting to let on that a part of him was scared to death.

Later, Zeke and Danny hiked back up to their house and sat, once again, at their kitchen table. They indulged in a couple of joints when they arrived. They were getting very drunk and very stoned.

They both had a lot on their minds and didn't speak much. They figured out how to get the plants back to Clayton and had pretty much solved the issue of the goo-soaked pot. Now, they needed to decide what to do with the body of the naked man in their weed field, who had already been dead for days before crossing their path.

"Jesus Christ! Let's just take him out to the old junkyard and burn him." Zeke finally gave in. He wasn't thrilled with the idea, but what else could they do without being caught and looking like grave robbers?

"The junkyard? Is that a smart idea? Is there nowhere else we can burn that thing?" Danny questioned.

"I don't know of any other place. We sure as shit don't want to be burning some zombie body around here. That would draw too much attention!" Zeke stood up from the table and walked toward the door. "But we aren't doing it tonight. We'll shove that thing in the shed, and when it gets dark again, we'll get it, take it to the junkyard, and set it ablaze!"

***

The painful hike back down to the pot field was damn near unbearable. It wasn't as easy as it seemed when they went earlier. Both brothers had sores on their feet, not to mention they were exhausted—mentally and physically. They knew there was no way around it. They had to put the thing on lockdown in the Hut as soon as possible.

When they reached the field, they walked to where the body was lying and dragged it into the little building. They brought an old tarp to cover it with.

The body stunk. The stench made Danny and Zeke gag the whole time they were around it. At one point, Danny gagged so hard that he swallowed his chew. Then, he puked it right back up. It burned both ways.

"Goddamn! That thing smells like the worst roadkill!" Danny said as they locked up the Hut.

"Yeah. You see where the flesh was starting to droop off of it? I thought I was for sure going to puke...like, you did." Zeke chuckled.

"Very funny, asshole! I only puked because I swallowed my chew."

"I'm sure that was the only reason."

Danny and Zeke were just about to get back on the trail to head back to the house when something dawned on Zeke. He stopped in his tracks and turned to head back down to the field.

"Where the fuck are you going?" Danny seemed aggravated. He just wanted to go home and go to bed.

Zeke was already far from the trail, but his voice was clear. "Those buds that got covered in that shit...we need to get what we can and hang them up to dry!"

"Really? Now?" Danny followed suit and headed away from the trail to catch up with his brother. By the time he caught up, Zeke was already starting to collect as many buds from the plants as he could, gathering them in his shirt.

"Just do what I am doing. We'll get what we can and put them in the Hut. Then we can go home. Let's make this quick, though. I know we are both fucking tired."

It only took the brothers about thirty minutes to get as many buds as possible. They unlocked the Hut and opened the door. The smell of the rotting corpse hit them both in the face. It was stronger than before. Zeke flipped the lights on and lifted the tarp to make sure the corpse was still 'dead.' It was. The body looked different, though, like it was bloating up—quickly. The flesh was bubbling. It resembled a stew made of remains and feces. Tiny boils on the body popped one by one. Green goo and liquid crimson burst from each one.

"Jesus..."

"What is it?" Danny was unloading his shirt and putting the stems of buds on a clothesline. From the look on his brother's face, he knew something was wrong.

"This thing looks like it's gonna explode." Zeke pinched his nose to block the stench. "We need to hurry the fuck up!"

They got all the stems of fresh bud hung as fast as they could. Syrupy beads of green dripped from everything they hung up. It got all over everything. By the time they were finished, they were covered in it.

"We might want to wash our asses good when we get back to the house!" Danny exclaimed. "I would hate to see what would happen if we forgot and got this shit in our eyes or mouth."

Zeke nodded.

After covering the boil-festering corpse again, the brothers continued back up the trail to get home. By this time, they were more exhausted than they had been in a while. They both were trying to keep calm the best they could. However, as they thought about everything that could happen if shit was to hit the fan, their anxiety levels started to rise.

"We're fucked, aren't we?" Danny stood in front of the doorway to his bedroom. He turned to Zeke.

"Nah. No worries, little brother. We'll get everything squared away. Go get some sleep." Zeke smirked as they both walked into their separate bedrooms.

***

Morning came quickly. The sun's rays beaming into Zeke's room from the cracks in the blinds woke him up instantly. "Son of a bitch!"

He rose from his bed, thrashing his arms and legs like a child throwing a fit, kicking his covers onto the floor. He followed his covers, turning over and plummeting to the ground.

Danny woke up and heard a loud THUD from his brother's room. He dashed from his room, running to Zeke's room. He laughed when he saw Zeke wrapped in blankets, looking like a baby curled up on the floor beside his bed.

"What the hell happened to you?" Danny asked.

"What's it look like? I fell out of bed. That damn sun beat right down on my eyes. Hell, I barely slept and only got comfortable a little while ago. How are you up so early?" Zeke replied as he threw his covers back on his bed. He leaned against the bed frame while sitting halfway on the mattress.

"I had trouble sleeping too. Kept having nightmares about zombies and monsters and shit like that. Hard to have those kinda' dreams, knowing what is out in the Hut." Danny suddenly stopped; his voice became serious. "So, what is the plan?"

Zeke stretched his arms and hopped up from the floor. "The plan? The plan is to burn that body at the junkyard and hope those buds are dry. After that, we'll see what happens."

Zeke's cell phone rang. He looked around and found his jeans lying on the end of the bed. He could see the light of his phone blinking through the pocket. He grabbed his jeans and fished out the phone. "Shit. Clayton."

He took a deep breath and pushed the ANSWER button. He was about to say what one usually does when answering the phone, but Clayton's voice spoke up first.

"Zeke, how is everything going with what we talked about? I would hate to put a hurtin' on you and your brother."

"Clayton, hey! Yeah, everything is going fine. We will have your plants and a little more for ya in a couple of days."

"Tomorrow."

Zeke was thrown off. "Tomorrow?"

"Yeah, tomorrow. I need everything I'm owed. Some strains are going with a big buyer, which is why I don't need to worry about you and tweedle-dumb fucking up my shit." Clayton had an intense way of speaking with his thick southern drawl. When he said he was going to hurt you, he wasn't kidding. Those who knew him understood. Some never got the hint until it was too late.

"Everything will be taken care of by tomorrow then. I just thought we had an extra day." Zeke could hear Clayton's voice turn into a twisted-sounding chuckle.

"An extra day? Boy, you know I don't fuck around." Clayton let out a chilling laugh, then hung up.

Zeke and Danny looked at each other with worry. It was starting to seem, to the brothers, like they were fucked.

"Well, let's get to the Hut and take care of all of this," Zeke ordered.

Neither one of them wanted to walk back down the trail again. They'd already walked back and forth too many times in a short period, and their feet couldn't take much more.

Upon reaching the Hut and the weed field, Danny started getting a bad feeling. The sun was shining, and the plants all looked great out in the field. Something in his head told him the peace was too good to be true.

"Got a bad feeling coming on, Zeke."

"Bad feeling? How so?" Zeke asked as he unlocked the door to the Hut.

"Yeah, I don't know why. I just have a bad feeling."

Zeke shook his head and laughed, trying to stay positive and keep his brother thinking positively. As soon as he flipped the lights on in the Hut, all positivity went out the window.

"What the fuck?" Danny hollered as he and Zeke stepped further inside.

With the lights on, they saw the disgusting mess within their little building of buds. It appeared the corpse, which was bloated and bubbling the last time they checked on it, had exploded! Pieces of rotted flesh hung from the ceiling and dripped into puddles of mush on the floor. Green ooze was splashed everywhere, soaking every bud in the room. The smell made Danny's weak stomach want to unleash whatever it held. Zeke gagged every few seconds.

"Holy shit! That thing blew up!" Danny exclaimed.

"Looks that way," Zeke replied. A nasty slab of rotten meat slid off the ceiling and landed on his head. "Dammit!" He hollered, grabbing the flesh sliding down his forehead, and tossing it aside.

"Now, this is a problem," Danny added.

Zeke gritted his teeth furiously and walked around the room, surveying the mess. All the ready buds were soaked. He imagined himself and his brother being brutally buttfucked by one of Clayton's goons, then skinned alive before being fed to hogs.

"Fuck it!" Zeke shouted. He walked to one of the mini-fridges and grabbed a box of sandwich bags sitting on top. "We are bagging all of this up and delivering as is. We'll just hope this shit dries out better by tomorrow."

"What about the plants?" Danny wondered out loud.

"Go out to the field, grab the plants from the ready row, and get to cutting. He may not be getting full plants, but he will get what he wants off them, if not more," said Zeke, already bagging weed.

Danny grabbed a handful of baggies and walked out to the field. He did as told and grabbed what he could, picking and cutting buds from full plants. It took a couple of hours for them to gather everything they needed. They had to stop at one point to run to the house for more baggies and grocery bags.

In time, they bagged all the cannabis they could and cleaned the Hut to the best of their ability. They knew there was much left to do, but at least they didn't need to worry about where to hide the rotting corpse anymore.

***

Danny and Zeke spent the rest of the day getting everything they owed Clayton in order. They started their usual ritual of smoking and drinking after a hard day's work. Zeke grabbed a six-foot bong from the kitchen closet. He was about to load the bowl with a hard-to-find strain from his private stash when Danny stopped him.

"Here's an idea..." Danny pulled a goo-soaked bud from one of the bags and grinned. "What if we try one of these?"

"I don't know, Dan. What if that shit is just straight poison and kills us?"

"Honestly, I don't think it will do anything. I mean, it's one of the dryer buds, and maybe we will get, like, super high," he said, breaking the infected bud up with his fingers. It crumbled nicely onto the table.

"I dunno..."

Seeing Zeke so worried about smoking weed was different. Danny took a couple of pinches from the table and placed the crumbled buds into the bong's bowl. Neither said a word as He pulled the bong towards himself. Zeke watched, curious about what might happen.

"Here goes nothin'!" Danny hollered as he put his lighter to the bowl, filling the chamber with smoke. He looked up at Zeke, pulled the stem from the bong's base, and inhaled. His eyes instantly became red and swollen.

Danny's coughing fit was hard to watch; it didn't make Zeke want to try the shit. When Danny slid the bong over to him, he declined by pushing it back. "I can't, man. The way you're hacking from one rip—no, thank you. My lungs would collapse."

"Really?" Danny wasn't pleased by Zeke's decision, but he felt the power of the smoke. His head was light as a feather, and he felt like his body was lifting off the floor. "Fuck it!" He said and gave the bong another rip. This time, when he coughed, he hocked a wet, black wad from his throat.

"Gross! I wouldn't hit that shit anymore, bro! That loogy looks like it might come alive. Glad I passed on it." Zeke knew smoking this weed was a bad idea. He wished he had stopped Danny.

"Whatever, I just wanted to try it. I mean, we try every strain we encounter. Might as well try this, too." When Danny finished speaking, he coughed again, hacking up more black jelly.

"Danny, you, okay?" Zeke asked, feeling concerned. He walked over and gave Zeke a pat on the back, trying to calm his cough. "Try to breathe, man," he said as Danny put his head down on the table.

Danny's breathing became heavy and rapid. Zeke's sense of worry verged on panic.

"I don't feel so great," Danny said in a weak voice. He put his hands on the table and placed them under his forehead. His body started shaking. The shakes quickly evolved into full-blown convulsions.

"Danny?"

Danny didn't respond.

Danny? Bro, you okay?" Zeke asked. His hands were on his brother's shoulders.

The convulsing stopped, and Danny's breathing went back to normal. Zeke felt relieved. He backed off to give Danny some breathing room, and within a matter of seconds, BOOM!

Danny slammed his forehead on the table. Then he did it again. Zeke ran to him and tried to hold his head. Danny was too strong. He kept slamming his head—over and over—until the table splintered. Blood poured from the growing number of contusions. Crimson smeared the table with every hit.

"Goddamn! Danny! Stop!" There didn't seem to be anything Zeke could do. He shoved Danny, knocking him from the seat.

Danny was face down on the floor, not moving. Zeke knelt beside him and put his hand on Danny's back. "Danny?" He could hear his brother breathing heavily again. "Danny? You cool, man?"

Danny lifted his head. His eyes were bleeding. Black sludge poured from his nose and mouth. Veins popped from his face as his skin turned gray. He looked up, giving Zeke a nasty glare, then spit in his face. Saliva and black dripped from his wicked grin.

Zeke jumped back.

Zeke ran out of the kitchen and up the stairs to his bedroom. He could hear Danny downstairs, breaking stuff. Monstrous screams and hideous laughter also echoed throughout the house.

Zeke's mind raced. He didn't know what he should do. Any situation in which he was threatened usually ended with him beating the hell out of someone, but this was his brother. What was he going to do? Was there a cure? He would never forgive himself if he hurt his brother and found out there was a cure.

Danny's heavy footsteps thundered up the stairs.

Zeke had to make a decision.

"Zeeeeke!" Danny hissed. "Just me, Zeeeeeke!" There was a horrible giggle in his words.

At that moment, Zeke knew he was no longer dealing with his brother. Zeke also realized he needed to act fast. The old Louisville Slugger in the corner of his room came to mind. He quickly grabbed it and waited. The heavy footsteps of the thing that used to be his brother stopped in front of his bedroom door.

"Zeeeke...I know you're in theeeeerre."

Zeke heard gargling in the creature's throat as it hissed at him. He raised the bat over his head, prepared to bring it down as soon as the door opened. The doorknob slowly turned. Sweat dripped from Zeke's brow. The door opened inch by inch. As soon as it fully opened, he charged, bringing the bat down. The impact caused the shell of his brother's head to split open. Green slosh painted the walls. The creature fell backward as Zeke fell to the floor. Its head went through the drywall.

"This can't be happening."

In disbelief, Zeke watched as this monstrous, reanimated version of Danny pulled its head from the wall. Without hesitating, Zeke brought the bat down repeatedly on its head. The attack didn't seem to faze it. It kept hissing. Zeke just kept bashing. Then he noticed something: the monster's blood flying all over his room was a dark green. It was like the ooze that came out of Thomas Jenkins when he got shot.

After three minutes of beating the living shit out of his brother's head, the bat splintered. Zeke was splattered with goo from head to toe. Every time he brought the bat down on its head, he got more drenched. He watched as his brother's head split in two and smashed on top. It started twitching.

Zeke couldn't take anymore. He went to his room again, grabbed the pistol from his desk, and then walked back out to face his mutated, mutilated brother. Shooting twice, he put a round into his brother's chest and one in his head. The twitching stopped. "No way! No fucking way!"

Zeke ran to the shell that was once his brother to make sure he was finally dead. He checked to see if there was any sign Danny was still breathing. There wasn't. He was dead.

Goo drizzled through the cracks of the floor. Zeke could hear it drip onto the floor below. He grabbed a blanket and covered his brother's mangled corpse.

***

A feeling of psychosis crept up on Zeke. He didn't move his brother from where he lay—just left him there, covered up. Instead, he walked downstairs, found the good whiskey, and twisted the cap off. With a couple of strong chugs, half the bottle was gone. He leaned against the kitchen counter and searched for a pack of smokes; he wasn't much of a smoker unless he was having a drink. Considering what he'd been dealing with, he felt a smoke would go nicely with the whiskey.

A loud knock sounded at the front door.

"What now?" Zeke sighed. The front door had a big window, but the frosted pattern in the glass made it difficult to see through. Zeke could tell someone was on the other side—just not *who*. He opened the door swiftly. "Can I help you?" He asked a man standing in the shadows.

"Well, I guess that all depends," Out of the darkness came a slender man. He was dressed in black and had a twisted grin. "I was passing by and heard some noises. I figured I would come make sure everything was okay."

Zeke sighed, relieved it hadn't been Clayton waiting for him on the other side of the door. Relief turned to confusion. "Yeah, thanks. It was just a big rat. I had to chase it around the house." He laughed nervously.

The man in black raised his brow. "Is that so?" he asked in a tone suggesting he knew damn well that Zeke was full of shit.

"Yeah, they recently got bad around here and made their way into the house." Zeke laughed again.

"Hmmm...okay then." He stood at the door, grinning at Zeke. "Well, I guess there's nothing I can do to help then." He pulled a cigarette from the breast pocket of his black shirt and placed it between his lips. He was about to light it when he noticed Zeke staring at the nicotine stick. "You need one? You look like you could use one," the man asked.

Zeke stood there for a second, wondering if he really wanted one or not. "Yeah, what the hell. I could use one."

The man pulled the pack from his pocket and held it out. Before Zeke could grab it, the man pulled it back. He gave another big grin. "I tell you what..." The man pulled a cigarette from the pack. "Why don't you share some of that whiskey you got there, and you can have as many as you want. Sound good?"

"Whiskey? Haven't been drinking." Zeke tried to lie.

The man laughed. "Oh, don't be stupid. I can smell the booze on you from down the street!" He squinted; his right brow went up. "How about I just be blunt?"

Zeke wanted to get pissed. However, there was something about the man in the black that made him feel uneasy. "Go right ahead."

"Well, what if I told you that you should probably invite me in for a drink or two before you find yourself in a very, very bad situation?" The man took a long drag off his cigarette and smiled.

"What's this about?" Zeke asked.

"How about I come in and we have a little chat?" The man replied.

When Zeke started to open the door more, the man pushed it open and walked past. He headed toward the kitchen, pausing in the living room to wait for Zeke.

"So, what's this about?" Zeke asked again, more forcefully this time.

He watched nervously as a string of goo from his brother's mangled corpse dripped from the ceiling above, landing near where the man in black stood.

The man shook his head. "How about that drink first?"

They went into the kitchen. The man took a seat at the table. Zeke poured each of them glasses of whiskey, then sat across from him.

"Here." Zeke handed him the glass, not seeming too thrilled.

"How kind of you." The man took a big sip from the glass. He then handed the cigarette across the table over to Zeke. "That's good shit!" he said before letting out a disgustingly loud belch.

Zeke nodded, agreeing with the man.

"So! Let's get down to business, shall we?" The man excitedly hollered out. "You see, in case you haven't figured it out just yet, it is no accident that I am here."

"I kind of figured."

"Yeah. See, I know a lot more than you seem to realize," the man said, sipping from his glass again.

"Yeah? How so?" Zeke asked with a smirk.

"Oh, well, you see, I know you owe a man by the name of Clayton some plants." He scratched his neck, lifting his head but never taking his eyes off Zeke.

"Holy Shit! I knew it! You work for Clayton!" Zeke shouted.

The man laughed. "Not really, but he is an associate of mine. If anything, he works for me and, well, my boss...but that's another story." He took a long drag from his cigarette and put it out in the overflowing ashtray in the middle of the table.

"Look, I told Clayton I would have what he needs by tomorrow, and I will!"

Zeke's pleading seemed to amuse the man.

"Well, you better, young man! Or scary Mister Clayton is going to put a hurting on that ass!" The man in black grinned.

"Huh?" Zeke replied, thrown off by the man's demeanor.

The man cracked up. "Shit, kid! I am just fucking with you—well, kinda'. I mean, he won't whoop your bottom. He'll just feed it to his livestock." He struggled to quit laughing, seeming to enjoy Zeke's fearful expression.

"Wonderful."

"Oh, hey! It's not all bad."

"How so?"

"You could have turned into some fucked up thing out of a Romero flick—like your brother!" The man in black's words were mean but sincere. He had a good point.

"How the fuck did you know about that?" Zeke scooted his seat back from the table, preparing to lunge.

"Kid, whatever the hell you're thinking of doing... don't. I really don't feel like putting my fist through your head.

Zeke couldn't stand it anymore. Every time the man in black opened his mouth, Zeke got angrier. The man's smugness didn't help. He was about to lose his shit and wished the stranger would get to the point or leave. Usually, he was pretty good at keeping cool, but with everything that had happened, he was at the end of his rope. As it grew more difficult to deal with things rationally, it became easier to get annoyed. "Oh yeah? What makes you so sure of yourself, Mister?"

The man in black looked down at his breast pocket, where he kept his cigarettes. One of the cigarettes rose from his pocket without him using any hands. It slowly poked from the top of the pocket, making its way out and floating to the man's mouth.

"How in the fuck did you do that?" Zeke asked with wide eyes.

"Some would say magic, but that would be bullshit. Just years of experience." The man cracked a twisted smile. "Look, Kid! I'm not here to fuck you up unless you ignore me. Then, I might fuck you up." He raised his hand and pointed to the bottle of whiskey. "Another round would be good."

"So would another cigarette." Zeke grabbed the bottle around the neck and filled their glasses. The man tossed a cigarette in his direction. Zeke picked up the cigarette and put it in his mouth. Before he could grab a lighter, it seemed to light itself. "Seriously, how are you doing that?"

"Been in this business a while. You learn things." He downed the whole glass of whiskey and slammed it on the table. "Always good to have a drink with a friend! The last friend I drank with... had to blow his head off with a shotgun." The man cackled again, then quickly went back to being serious.

"So, why are you here right now?" Zeke inquired.

The man stretched his arms. A lit cigarette dangled from his lips, and smoke streamed from his nostrils. "You won't believe it, but I'm kind of here to help."

"You're right. I don't believe it." Zeke took a drag off his cigarette and stared intensely at the man sitting across from him.

"Look, you owe a very bad man some things you simply don't have. Unless you come up with everything, you're going to end up a pile of animal chow."

"What am I supposed to do then?" Zeke placed his hands on his head, running them through his black hair. "And who are you again?" He asked.

The man's smile went away. His face became serious. "First thing, you don't ask me questions. I ask the fucking questions, and I tell you what you need to do. If you decline, then that's on you. No more fucking questions!"

Zeke tried not to worry about who the man was and how he knew so much. He knew he needed to shut up and listen. "Gotcha," he replied after a short sigh.

"You need to realize the gold you have in your possession right now."

"What do you mean?"

"What made your brother change?"

Zeke thought for a second and understood what the man was talking about. "The weed?"

"Of course, the weed! It's a rare tool you have. If I were you, I would start thinking about how to use it to your advantage." The man stood up from the table. He walked back into the living room and headed for the front door.

"Wait...that's it?"

"What's it?"

"That's your advice on how to help me?" Zeke questioned.

The man chuckled. He turned to face Zeke, placing a hand on his shoulder. "Kid, if you can't figure out what to do, then I don't think there's any help for you."

***

With the sudden departure of the man in black, Zeke stood at the door and watched the man walk down the driveway and disappear. He struggled to wrap his head around the many situations at hand. How did the stranger in black know about everything? Why did he seem like he wanted to help? How the fuck did he do that trick with his cigarettes?

One thing he knew: he was screwed beyond belief if he didn't figure out a plan.

He went upstairs and stood in front of his brother's covered corpse. A tear rolled down his cheek as he fell to his knees. "I'm sorry, brother. I really am."

Pounding his fists on the floor, his sobs turned into a full-on breakdown. Life had never seemed so difficult. They had their troubles, like everyone. But in the past couple of days, everything flipped upside down and inside out.

It was a rough night. Zeke managed to get a little sleep. He mainly lay in bed, thinking about what the man in black said to him. He also thought about his game plan for meeting up with Clayton.

When the sun came up, it blasted into the room and woke Zeke up. This time, he wasn't as angry about it. He knew he needed to get some things in order and couldn't sleep in. He quickly got out of bed and headed down to the kitchen, running past the blanket covering Danny's body. There wasn't any beer left in the fridge, so he went for the whiskey instead.

After taking a few big gulps from the bottle, Zeke ran back upstairs to grab his boots. This time, he didn't run past his brother. He lifted the cover and stared at Danny's remains. His skin was turning dark and sprouting weird boils, much like the last undead creature. This worried Zeke, but there was no time to deal with it. He swiped the boots from his bedroom and ran down the stairs and out the back door.

Zeke was almost to the Hut when his cell phone rang. It was Clayton. He hesitated to answer at first but knew if he didn't, Clayton would call back even angrier.

"Hello?" he answered.

"Zeke, I hope everything is in order. It is, isn't it?" Clayton's voice was intimidating. It sounded like he was in a car.

"Yes. Everything is taken care of."

"Good to hear. We won't be long." Clayton hung up.

Zeke ran as fast as he could, reaching the Hut in record time. He brought a backpack, knowing he needed to carry as much as possible.

"Damn! Damn! Damn!"

When he arrived at the Hut, Zeke grabbed all the hanging buds and the trimmed buds in baskets and picked up anything he could find on the floor. The buds that were doused in the green goo had dried. The goo had turned the buds a darker shade of green with streaks of neon. It looked nice. He hoped the plan in his head was going to work.

He gathered everything quickly and jetted back to the house. He was out of breath and nervous when he reached the kitchen. Clayton would be there any second. It was crunch time.

Sure enough, there was a knock at the front door about fifteen minutes after Zeke got back to the house. His palms were sweaty, and he was struggling not to shake. Clayton was the kind of man who could smell fear and would use it to his advantage any way he could.

Zeke walked to the front door as one of Clayton's henchmen pounded his fist against it. Through the window, he could tell Clayton was standing in the middle. There were at least two men with him. He never went anywhere without back-up. Zeke slowly turned the knob and pulled the door open.

"Mister Clayton! Good to see you." Zeke tried brown-nosing.

"Oh, I'm sure you've been pacing back and forth around this shit-hole, wanting me to hurry up so you could see my pretty face." Clayton laughed, immediately switching back into serious mode. "Cut the shit, Zeke. Where's my shit?"

Zeke directed the men to come inside and have a seat. One man was slightly taller than him, wearing a black vest over a ragged, white undershirt. The other henchman wore a short-sleeved black t-shirt.

They sat on the couch while Clayton remained standing. He was a big man with a fluffy beard and long hair, usually kept in a ponytail.

"Now, I told you not to fuck me around. I expect you have listened," Clayton said, moving closer to Zeke.

Zeke nodded. "Of course! I'll be right back." He ran into the kitchen and gathered all the buds and the few plants he was able to bring up. He figured it would be enough to keep him alive—he hoped.

When Zeke returned to the living room, Clayton was looking around. The two henchmen were sitting quietly on the couch. Zeke walked in with the first few bundles of large bags full of cannabis. He set them down and returned to the kitchen. Clayton took notice and walked over to a chair next to the kitchen door. This shift in location startled Zeke when he came out with more bundles.

"Is this everything?" Clayton asked as Zeke brought the last bit into the living room and set it down.

"Yeah. I wasn't able to get all of the full plants you wanted, but I figured you would be okay as long as you got the same amount in trimmed bud," Zeke said confidently.

Clayton looked over everything, opening a few bags to get a good look at the product. He smirked and grabbed one of the larger buds from one of the bags containing the "infected" weed. He looked intrigued.

"That's a nice shade of green. Haven't seen that before." Clayton rolled the bud around in his hand and handed it to the henchman wearing the vest. "Try that."

"I don't have anything to smoke it with," the henchman said.

Zeke quickly stepped in. "I have something you can use! I have a couple of bongs, some wraps, and some papers. What Cha' prefer?"

"I like joints," The henchman said, sounding like a spoiled child.

"Get the boy a rolling paper, Zeke," Clayton ordered. He paused for a second and continued. "Hell, I could use a toke! Make it a J for all of us!"

Zeke nodded. "Coming right up!" He ran into the kitchen and grabbed the tray he kept his rolling stuff on. There was a pack of papers, a blunt wrap, and a few buds. The plan was in motion—no room for error. Knowing there was a good chance the product would be tested, he made sure he was prepared to roll a joint with no goo on it. After seeing the effects of that shit, keeping that smoke away from his lungs was key.

Sitting on the loveseat next to the henchmen, Zeke set the tray in his lap and got to work. He ground up an "infected" bud and rolled three joints. He snuck the one he'd already rolled from clean bud to the side. "Let's smoke!" He handed the tainted joints to the henchmen and Clayton.

Clayton looked unsure. "You all blaze up first. I wanna make sure that shit isn't some CBD bullshit." Clayton looked at Zeke. "I'm serious, Zeke. I will kill you if you fuck with my buzz."

One of the henchmen pulled out a red lighter, lit his joint, and inhaled deeply. The other henchmen followed suit. It wasn't long before the voodoo smoke began taking hold.

"Damn, I'm pretty stoned already, boss!"

"Yeah, this shit is pretty killer!" the other henchman exclaimed.

Zeke grabbed his joint off the tray and put it to his lips. He lit it and took a deep toke. Clayton squinted, staring hard at Zeke.

"You just roll that?" He asked.

Zeke exhaled and started choking. When he was able to catch his breath, he replied. "Yeah, didn't you see me? I'm a quick roller."

"That so?" Clayton replied, furrowing his brow quizzically. He reached over and grabbed the joint from Zeke's fingers. "Think I'll hit this one a couple of times!" Being the forceful prick he was, he took three good hits, then handed it back to Zeke.

"See, it's good shit," Zeke responded, giving a fake smile.

"Yeah, I'm definitely enjoying this," one of the henchmen added. The other nodded and kept hitting the joint.

Zeke started to worry as he watched the men go to town on the joints. He knew what might happen. He just wasn't sure when. Then he noticed the ceiling. Danny's remains were on the second floor right above him. Something red dripped down.

The first drip Zeke noticed fell behind Clayton's head, landing on the couch. His eyes widened as the drips continued every couple of seconds. He looked at the henchmen. They were too blazed to notice anything; one had fallen asleep, while the other was zoning out on a picture hanging on the wall—a hustler fold-out of a redheaded woman, half-clothed, with her fingers spreading her pussy lips open.

"Zeke, it appears this shit is pretty good," Clayton said with a smile. "I might be coming back for more, if possible," he added, fidgeting with his ponytail.

"I'm sure that won't be a problem." Zeke was shocked. Things seemed to be working out. As a matter of fact, they seemed to be working out a little too well. One thing bothered him since the smoking session began. When was the change going to happen? It hadn't taken Danny so long.

Clayton stood and smacked the sleeping henchman in the head. "Wake up, fuckwad! I got things to do!" The henchman nodded and got up. He was pretty fucked up. Clayton walked over to him and snapped his fingers in front of him. "Hey! Come on!"

All three men were headed toward the front door to leave when Clayton stopped and turned around.

"Something wrong?" Zeke asked.

Clayton squinted and combed his beard with his fingers. His face got serious. "Nah. Just tell your brother I said hi. I know he will hate that he missed me." He turned back around, and the three men walked out the door.

Zeke quickly ran up the stairs to investigate what was happening with Danny's bloated corpse. It was as bad as he figured. He pulled the tarp back and saw his brother's entire body was covered in huge boils. They were festering and looked ready to burst at any moment.

Zeke heard a commotion outside of the house. It sounded like Clayton screaming. Zeke ran to a window and looked out.

"Holy shit!"

As the men walked to their vehicle, the henchmen started to change. Clayton fought off both men, punching and swatting at them with a terrified look on his face. He reached into his jacket and pulled out a large hand cannon. He pointed it at the man in the vest and fired into his chest. It didn't matter. The henchman kept walking toward Clayton.

"You motherfuckers! What the hell is wrong with you?" Clayton hollered. "I swear, I am gonna beat you both black and blue!" He ignored the fact that he'd just blown a nice-sized hole into the man.

The henchman got closer. Clayton fired another shot, this time hitting the man in the shoulder. It didn't affect him. "What the..." He fired again. That was three shots. The man kept getting closer. "SON OF A BITCH!" He cocked the hammer back, about to fire a fourth shot. Before he could, the other henchman wrapped his arms around him and squeezed. Clayton dropped the gun but managed to slam the back of his head into the henchman's face. Blood spattered the back of Clayton's head, dripping off his long ponytail. The henchman let go, enabling Clayton to get free.

He took staggered back, frantically looking around for his gun—nowhere in sight. He glanced up at Zeke's house and dashed for the front door.

Zeke had watched the whole thing happen from the window. It was unclear to him exactly how it would go when Clayton burst in. He ran down the stairs just in time for the door to crash open. Clayton barreled in, showing signs of emotions he wasn't usually known for having. The color of his skin had drained from the fear, and he looked confused.

"Zeke, you wanna tell me what the fuck just happened out there? Both my men just attacked me!" He slammed the door behind him and locked it.

Zeke thought for a second, knowing the truth would make things worse. "I don't know," he said, raising his hands. He went to the living room window and peered out.

"Well, I don't know either. All I know is, I shot that motherfucker three times, and he kept coming for me!" Clayton stood next to Zeke at the window and looked out. Both henchmen were walking up the hill toward the house. Their skin was taking on a shade that looked green one minute and gray the next. "What the hell did you give them?"

Zeke turned to look at Clayton. "Nothing!" He started backing slowly away from Clayton.

"Was it the weed, Zeke? You try to poison us?" Clayton's tone was frightening. He lunged at Zeke.

"It wasn't the weed!" Zeke dodged Clayton's attack and darted for the stairs.

"I'm gonna rip your fucking eyes out!" Clayton screamed as he charged toward the stairs.

Zeke was almost at the top when he heard a sloshing sound. It was like someone—or something—was gargling. The smell in the upstairs hallway was worse than before. He glanced down the hall toward Danny and realized the source of the sound and stench. The bloated corpse appeared ready to burst as vile gasses wheezed and gurgled through fissures in the taut, rotten flesh.

As Zeke ran to find more stuff to cover his brother's cadaver with, Clayton came up from behind him, grabbed him by the neck, and threw him down.

"Goddamn!" Clayton exclaimed as he got a whiff of the stench. "You got a toilet problem or some—" Clayton's words trailed off when he noticed Danny's body against the wall. He walked past Zeke, who was on the floor, holding his throat, trying to catch his breath. "That's some nasty shit!" He got another hard whiff of the stench. He could taste chunks of his last meal, coming from his gut, through his throat, and filling his mouth. Vomit spewed past his lips, splashing everything in front of him.

Zeke looked up and saw Clayton retching and Danny's body. He knew what was about to happen. He got up from the floor as fast as possible and ducked into the closest room. He hastily slammed the door, but it bounced back open a crack.

"Can't hide from me!" Clayton hollered with anger in his eyes and puke dripping from his beard. He charged down the hall toward the room where Zeke hid.

"Shit!" Zeke exclaimed and shut the door the rest of the way. He hoped it would keep Clayton out.

Clayton pounded on the door, screaming at Zeke. Then he stopped and went silent. From the other side of the door, Zeke thought he heard something—like a balloon about to pop. He cracked the door just in time to see Danny's body explode. Clayton was pummeled to the floor by a torrent of green slime and rotten chunks of meat.

Zeke opened the door the rest of the way and walked out. Danny's body was mush. He noticed his brother's head a few inches from where Clayton lay. Taking a closer look, he realized Danny's head must have blown off with enough force to knock the big man unconscious.

"Holy fuck! Thanks, Dan." Zeke hurried down the steps, about to walk out the front door, then paused. The urge for a drink hit him. He glanced up the stairs. Clayton was still on his back, passed out on the floor. "Fuck it!" he said, running for the kitchen. He knew he needed to hurry. As he walked into the kitchen, he heard Clayton moving around upstairs. "Dammit."

Zeke headed straight to the fridge. The options were slim, and time was running out. The choices were generic cola, an old carton of orange juice, and beer. He grabbed the cola, then opened the ice box and pulled out a half-empty fifth of whiskey.

Beverages in hand, Zeke ran back to the living room. He heard a loud THUD and saw Clayton at the top of the stairs. He was covered in green slime and struggling in earnest to stand up.

"Oh fuck..." Zeke said to himself. He looked at the large amounts of cannabis on the floor, then looked back up at Clayton, who was now on his feet and pulling a pistol from the side of his pants. Zeke didn't have time to weigh the options. Should he grab as much weed as he could carry or get the hell out of there and come back for it later? He got the hell out of the house and took off running down the street.

***

In the house, Clayton walked down the stairs, gun in hand, mad as hell, grumbling things under his breath as he headed toward the living room. He mainly mumbled about the horrible things he would do to Zeke when he caught up with him.

"I swear to fuck, I am gonna rip that son of a bitch's throat out—maybe let one of my

freaks have their way with him beforehand!"

All he could see was a dark shade of red.

***

Zeke ran as fast as he ever had down the road. He wasn't sure where he was going but knew he needed to hide. No one crossed Clayton and survived. Zeke knew Clayton would quickly head his way and take him out. Zeke didn't know that Clayton had other plans before he went gunning for Zeke.

***

Like Zeke, the first thing Clayton did was run to the fridge out of thirst. And, like Zeke, he grabbed a cola. Instead of taking it with him, he popped the tab and chugged it in seconds. The cool, crisp flavor was so satisfying that he grabbed another and chugged it as well. When he was finished, he threw the can across the kitchen, ready to find Zeke and destroy him.

***

About thirty minutes down the road, Zeke came across a rundown gas station. It appeared to still be a working gas station. Zeke figured decided to go inside and scope it out. A couple of people were looking out at him from the front window. He gave a wave and a slight smile and walked toward the building.

When he walked in, the two people who glared at him from the window were now staring holes through him. The man behind the counter looked to be in his mid-fifties. He was balding and had a scraggly beard.

"Boy, you look as if you have been through some shit!" The man behind the counter shouted, then hooted in laughter.

"He definitely looks as if he has been into some shit!" The other older man station added.

"What can we do for you this fine afternoon?" The man behind the counter asked.

Zeke quickly looked out the window and turned back to the man. "Well, if you have a phone, that would be great..."

"A phone? Needin' to call someone?" The other man chuckled.

"Yeah. I imagine that is what they're around for... for calls." It was apparent that Zeke didn't find the comment funny. He just wanted to call a friend and get out of the area before Clayton found him.

"There is a pay phone in the back. Have at it!" The man behind the counter barked.

Zeke nodded and walked toward the back. He couldn't recall if he had ever been to this gas station. He and his brother had lived in the area for the better part of their lives, and he couldn't remember ever seeing it before. *Weird*, he thought as he reached for the phone.

He hoped to reach a friend who worked at a bar nearby. She was always good for bailing him out of sticky situations when he managed to fuck himself. The line just rang and rang.

"Dammit, Steph! Pick up! What the hell?"

Zeke hung up and thought for a minute about who else to call. He thought for sure Stephanie would answer and save the day. Not this time. His mind was blank. He didn't have many people he considered actual friends. Most of his so-called friends just needed smoke or a place to get drunk and crash. It bothered him more than he ever let on. No one was coming to save the day. It didn't help he was getting bad vibes from how the old men, especially the cashier, glared at him.

Just then, the gas station door opened. He feared it was Clayton.

"Hey, fellas! How is business today?"

Zeke realized the voice was not one he was fearful of. He walked toward the front and recognized the man speaking. It was the man in black who came by the house earlier.

"Hey!" Zeke hollered.

The man in black and the other two men turned and looked in his direction. The man in black grinned and chuckled. He moved closer to Zeke.

"Well, hello there, Sport. How are things?" The man in black placed his hand on Zeke's shoulder. "Kinda' looking like you may need some help at this point. Am I right?" he asked.

Zeke took a deep breath. "Well, to be perfectly fucking honest, I am not doing so hot. That crazy-ass, Clayton, will most likely be here any moment and probably make me food for his livestock."

The man in black nodded. "Seems like you may need to call a lifeline."

"I tried. The only friend who would help me out is at work and not answering her calls right now." Zeke locked eyes with the man, unable to look away. There was something strange about this guy—more than he already realized.

"Work, huh?" The man in black puckered his lips and nodded again. "Where does she work?" he asked curiously.

"I don't see why that matters, but she works over at that bar, Max's," Zeke replied, confused.

"Max's? Well, I was there earlier, and let me tell you, they may be dealing with other things more important than phone calls right now." The man in black chuckled.

Zeke became defensive. "Did something happen? Did you do something there?"

"Boy, you ask a lot of questions!" The man replied. "I did nothing!"

Zeke sighed.

"However, someone else did something. Frankly, I don't know what happened after I left, but you shouldn't worry too much." The man grabbed a pack of smokes from his breast pocket, pulled a cigarette out, and tossed it into his mouth.

"Oh, you're not gonna have it light itself this time?" Zeke remarked.

The man grinned as the cigarette lit itself.

"Figures," Zeke said, rolling his eyes.

"So, you need a ride?" the man in black asked as he took a big drag from his cigarette.

Zeke didn't want to admit it but knew he needed help. "Yeah, I guess. I can't really say no at the moment, huh?"

"I guess not. Come on!" the man in black said aggressively, grabbing Zeke by the neck and pushing him in front of him. "The cars out front. Go ahead and get in. I'll be out there in a minute. Gotta take care of something real quick."

The situation was sticky, but Zeke felt listening to this guy was in his best interest. He did what he was told and headed out the door. Sitting at pump number three was a black Mustang. It took Zeke a minute to process the fact that the man in black hadn't had a vehicle earlier. To ask would risk pissing him off as well as possibly learning something he wished he hadn't. At this point, Zeke saw no reason to question things.

***

Meanwhile, in the gas station, the man in black stood at the counter. He gave both older men a grin. They gave each other a confused glance.

"Paul, how have things been since your wife passed?" The man in black asked the man behind the counter. The man behind the counter glanced at his buddy in confusion.

"Hey, do I know you, friend?" The man behind the counter asked with a snarl in his voice.

The man in black grinned, staring at the man behind the counter, whom he referred to as Paul, and hit his cigarette again.

Paul glared at the man in black with haste. He wasn't quite sure what the man was getting at, but he didn't like it. "Look here, you fuck face! I loved my wife!" he shouted.

The man in black laughed. "Is that why you bashed in her head while you anally fucked her with a curling iron? Then you blamed it on some poor asshole who got life in prison. That unlucky fella ended up hanging himself."

The man behind the counter was speechless. Images of his wife bent over with a bag over her head while he violently raped her anus with a hot curling iron. The pain in her screams still resonated in his head on most days. At that very moment, every emotion flooded back from that day. Snapping himself from the quick trip down memory lane, he continued to play stupid. "Wait just a minute! My wife died many years ago in a break-in on our home!"

"Yeah. Some break-in! The only reason you got away with jack or shit was because you're buddies with Sheriff Speaks. That old jack-off can barely read, let alone collect evidence. No. The truth is, yeah, there was a fucking break-in at your place. However, you planned the damn thing. You had that poor sap of a human come into your home and help you rape and torture that sweet old woman who gave you her all for so many years. You paid that dumb fuck to do the whole thing, but you got greedy. You fucking slammed that thing into your wife's backdoor, made sure it was good and hot, too. You even tried to open the hair-care machine while still inside her ass. You laughed hysterically, smothering her with a plastic bag, beating her face until blood reconstructed her face. Such a piece of shit." The man in black laughed hysterically.

"Hey! He loved his wife. Who the hell are you to come in here and make these accusations?" The other man spoke up.

"Yeah, you should probably shut the fuck up, Brody! We all know why you haven't been married in years, you paedophile fuck!" The man in black put his hand in his pocket and pulled out a photograph. "This ring any bells?"

"How did you...?" The other old man asked, sweating. "I don't know where you got that, but it was a long time ago!" His voice shook as he spoke, fear attached to his words. "I don't know how you got that photo. I don't know why you have that photo, but it's all bullshit!" Brody wiped the sweat from his brow while tears filled his eyes.

"Bullshit? Ha! You are one of the worst paedophiles in a hundred miles!" The man in black took a drag off his cigarette. "Dammit! I am really getting tired of this always being the case!" he shouted. "I have so much more going on, and shit always has to fucking happen all at once!" He rubbed his eyes with his palms, letting out a roar as he did so.

"What the hell you mean, Mister?" Brody inquired.

"I mean that I am just going to get to the point here!" The man in black took another big drag from his cigarette. The photo he'd shown to Brody had fallen to the floor. The man in black glanced down at the horrific Polaroid. The image of three grown men ganging up on a girl who couldn't have been more than thirteen turned his stomach. Looking back up in Brody's direction, he exhaled a cloud of smoke into Brody's face.

"Hey, you son of a bitch!" Brody hollered.

"You have gotten away with so much for so many years. You were told you would get what's coming to you, and the time is nigh!" The man in black turned his whole body to face him directly. "Brody, you have been the reason for so many tragedies. Families were torn apart because of your goddamn deeds. Children's innocence was stolen from them. Many of your victims later committed suicide, you fucking pig! You thought you were in the clear. Now you know you only got away with it for a while." He pulled a small pistol from his back pocket and pointed at Brody's face. "Here's your punishment!" He pulled the trigger..., and out popped a little flag. "Gotcha!"

Brody jumped at the toy gun POP! After the initial shock, he thought about lunging at the man in black. As he caught his breath, he wondered if he had anything to lose. "What the hell is your problem, Mister?" screamed Brody.

"What is wrong with me?" The man in black scoffed. "I'll make this easy."

At that moment, Brody came to a sudden stop before he could get near the man in black. He loosened his collar as a wave of heat struck him. Sweat rushed from every pore of his body.

"What the hell?" He shouted. The flesh of his face began melting. His skin looked like hot wax as it fell from the bone. Blood formed a large puddle where he stood. The shrieks that came from his mouth weren't only his own. The screams of his victims echoed in the room as well. When it was all said and done, Brody was no longer a person. He took the form that was always meant for him—a big pile of shit. A pile of ruined clothes intermingled with a mound of human waste occupied the space he had stood in moments before.

"What are you?" Paul asked, having pissed himself.

"Me? Oh, well, I'm not really anybody. I'm everybody. I'm the one who isn't Heaven or Hell. I'm not good, and I'm not bad. I am the perfect in-between—perfect enough to decide where shitbags like you end up!" the man in black preached, smiling down at the bubbling heap that was once Brody.

Shaken up, Paul started weeping. "I didn't mean to kill her!" he cried out. "It was a fucking accident!"

"God be damned! You are one shitty liar!" The man in black took his cigarette from his lips and threw it to the floor. "It doesn't matter. Say what you want. I know the truth, shithead!"

The man behind the counter frowned, starting to scratch at his eyes. He let out a loud yelp as he felt his own nails dig into his eyeballs. One of his hang nails snagged part of his left eye, slicing it down the middle. His screams were horrible, but his begging was more excruciating to hear. "I don't deserve this!" Paul cried.

"Don't deserve this? On the contrary. You very much deserve this and more!" The man in black grinned. He stared Paul in the face, giving him a wink.

The pain got more severe as a dark shade of red rose from his skin, causing his flesh to tear open. He clawed at his eyes with more aggression.

"See. Just because you got away with your murderous behavior for so long doesn't mean that you won't be held accountable for your actions at some point!"

Paul continued screaming as he pulled his eyes from their sockets. Blood poured from the raw cavities. His wailing sounded like a cat being raped by a bull as his body convulsed. Casting one last eyeless glance toward the man in black, he fell to the floor—a foamy red substance splashed from his sockets upon impact.

"Well, my work here is done," the man in black stated, smirking as he surveyed the mess at his feet.

***

The man in black walked out to his Mustang. Zeke was waiting patiently in the front passenger seat. The man walked over to the pump and started pumping gas into the vehicle. He peered in the window at Zeke. "Hey, I could use a burger! You hungry!"

Zeke looked confused. "I mean, I could use some grub."

"I'd say so. How much did you smoke today?" The man in black joked.

I mean, I could smoke more," Zeke replied.

The man in black got in the driver's seat and turned the key in the ignition. The engine roared to life, and the radio came on. A song by The Animals was playing. "You like classic rock?" he asked Zeke.

"Yeah."

"Good."

Zeke and the man in black drove away from the gas station, tunes blaring. Zeke looked at the man in black as he drove. He was hesitant to ask the question he had stewing. "Wouldn't have any weed on you, would you?"

The man in black grinned and reached into his middle console, pulling out a joint as thick as his thumb. Zeke pulled his lighter out, ready to be passed the stick.

"This shit, kid, will fuck you up!" the man in black stated.

Zeke took the joint and lit it, coughing as he inhaled the first stream of smoke to hit his lungs. "So, where are we going?" Zeke looked out in front of the vehicle. There, in the middle of the road, was a damn goat. It stood there, minding its own business, waiting to be hit like it didn't have a care in the world as the Mustang sped toward it. "Shit!" he shouted, thinking they were seconds away from making roadkill.

The man in black swerved to the left. "Damn him," he muttered under his breath.

"That was random," Zeke said.

The man in black laughed. "That was Gus. He never sleeps. He's a real annoying pain in the ass!"

"Gus?" Zeke questioned under his breath.

"Yeah, he is a real pain in the ass," The man in black repeated.

"Huh?" Zeke was becoming weary of being in the car with the mysterious man in black. However, something told him he needed to stay put. So, he did. He shook his head and puffed away on the joint.

"Hey, don't get too comfy. Clayton is coming for you, and I don't see him stopping anytime soon. May want to think of what some would call a plan," he said, laughing.

They drove down the road, passing the joint back and forth, blasting rock 'n' roll hits of the seventies. Zeke still didn't know what to think. He saw the image of his brother's rotting corpse coming at him and knew the weed was the cause. He didn't know what to believe anymore.

The man in black laughed like a madman as he drove. Somehow, Zeke was able to get comfortable in the cramped front seat. One last thought went through his head before he passed out:

Where's Clayton?

NOPE. THIS ISN'T THE END, MY FRIEND.
KEEP YOUR EYES PEELED FOR VOLUME TWO.

ABOUT THE AUTHOR

Chuck Nasty came from the womb with his middle fingers up!
He may be from the blue grass state, however, make no mistake about
it, he's here to make sure the red still flows.
When he isn't working on writing projects, he plays drums and does
main vocals for the two piece sludge band Bastard Sons of a Judas
Goat and does the podcast thing on: Nasty Nation, video store clerks
podcast and Graveyard Talk.
The authors that inspire Chuck are: Stephen King, Clive Barker, Ed-
ward Lee, RL Stine, Chuck Palahniuk and Hunter S Thompson.

HOUSE OF FLESH

Moving to a new home can be exciting. For one happy couple and their pothead friend, the excitment they get is more than they wanted. Erik Sutton decides to purchase a house without his long tome girl-friend, Lisa summers and his best friend, Judd. Never taking a look at it. They soon find out from the sexy and sketchy realtor, Victoria Dunn, that their new home has a disturbing past: Satanic orgies, disgusting creatures, blood, guts and temptation.

Much more awaits them, behind the many doors in the house of flesh.

THIRSTY?

A sinister soda machine in the middle of the forest...

What's the worst that can happen?

WARNING: This is an extreme read, some moments may offend the reader.

SLUDGE

From Stuart Bray, Jason Nickey, and Chuck Nasty comes Sludge!
Five tales of vomit inducing horror dealing with toxic waste, inhuman
creatures, altered biology, and squirmy parasites.
A perfect read for the dinner table!